TEMPORAL WILDCARDS AND RANDOM WALKS

A Collection of Short Stories

Michael Beauchamp

Eleusis Press

Temporal Wildcards and Random Walks

Copyright © 2016 by Michael Beauchamp

Published by Eleusis Press

2009 North 7th Street, Phoenix, Arizona, 85006

eleusisimages@gmail.com

Printed and bound in the United States of America

For Mom

Table of Contents

The Streets

The streets have secrets. They traverse a realm that belongs to the misunderstood, disenfranchised souls who wander the trash-strewn alleys and vacant lots of a world lying parallel to our own, a hidden universe of lost, desperate men, junkies and artists, broken messiahs and park bench philosophers. For the homeless, the streets are a jungle, a battlefield. Few people enter this world and escape to share their stories. Life on the streets is a difficult but simplified version of life in regular society. One imperative governs existence: survival.

Timothy MacGregor was, less than a year ago, a successful cog in the machinery of a prosperous advertising firm in a large, western Canadian city. He held a management position. He made a lot of money. He lived alone in a high-rise loft overlooking the ocean. He was fast becoming a legend in the competitive advertising market.

Timothy's social life was the envy of many of his peers. As a bachelor, he enjoyed all the pleasures and benefits of young success. He was a regular fixture on the downtown nightlife scene, cavorting with adoring women and consuming large amounts of booze and drugs.

In the early years of Timothy's escapades, substances were an exciting, even useful, aspect of his party lifestyle, total entertainment, celebratory and exploratory. In short time, however, Timothy developed a problem. Some people are able to use alcohol and narcotics liberally with no lasting, adverse consequences. Some become addicts. The mysterious combination of genetic and environmental influences that distinguishes the addict from the non-addict was present in Timothy's life. It was inevitable, with prolonged use, that he would eventually become an abuser. This happened much quicker than anyone could have predicted.

Cocaine was Timothy's drug of choice. He *loved* it. He loved the way it looked, all white and sparkly like the snow in a fairy tale. He loved playing with it, pushing around the powder with a razor blade on a small mirror. He loved the way it tasted when he snorted thick, expensive lines up his never-satiated nose. Most of all he loved the way it felt when it reached his brain and ignited the pure pleasure centers in his head like electrical storm microbursts.

The progression, the escalation, the erosion of Timothy's will – from the occasional line while out dancing to a nightly routine – transitioned from a daily ritual to an all-consuming obsession. Vials of powder gave way to pipes and lighters. Timothy went from crackhead to needle junkie, and downward still. Once a paragon of youthful success, he was now a frightening, cautionary story of tragedy and self-destruction.

Timothy lost his job, his home, and eventually his self-respect...but never his taste for the drug. Cocaine was his 'Ol' Reliable,' always there to pick him up when he needed it. His habit drew him to the streets, where, with a little ingenuity, he could sustain his consumption with an always-available supply of cheap and powerful chemicals.

Much like combat, survival on the streets, especially for an addict, depends on fellowship and on establishing and maintaining trustworthy relationships. Timothy tried to live as a loner during his early days of homelessness. Violence, ever present, lurking around every corner and at the end of every deal, soon found him.

"You ripped me off, man! There's no *way* that's a twenty piece." Timothy was in a filthy city park bathroom, arguing with a wiry, sketchy-looking character who had been the middleman in a small transaction, the kind of transaction that happens every few minutes in environments such as this. They were arguing over a tiny bag of crack cocaine. The white, rock-like substance was no larger than a pea, and even smaller than Timothy had expected.

"It is what it is," said the twitchy, scabby little man who had brought the drugs. He scratched at his jaw as he spoke. "Take it or leave it."

"I already gave you my money. What choice do I have?"

Timothy craved the drug. Despite his protests, he knew in his heart that he would indeed be taking the crack, rip-off or not, and consuming it as soon as he had a chance. He had been up for three days and nights already, smoking, swindling, scamming, and sinking ever-deeper into the depths of paranoid psychosis. He was desperate to stay high, desperate to avoid the inevitable crash of the comedown.

"Shit," Timothy said. He snatched up the bag of drugs and turned for the bathroom door, in his head already preparing his pipe and ready to take the next hit. "You little weasel," he said under his breath as he neared the door.

"What did you just say?" The runner had heard him. "Is there something you want to say to me? Say it to my face, goof."

Timothy then made a mistake. He turned to face the other man and said, "*You're* the goof," looking him directly in the eye.

The punch came swiftly and hit its mark precisely. For a little man, the runner could hit *hard.* The blow struck Timothy on the chin, on the 'button,' as pugilists like to say, rendering him unconscious instantly. Timothy collapsed in a heap before he knew what had happened. "Fool," said his attacker as he knelt and relieved Timothy of the drugs over which they had just argued.

Timothy languished in oblivion for close to an hour

before he awoke. On regaining consciousness, his first thought was concern for his drugs. With a panicky hand he clawed at his pockets and at the floor on which he lay. "That little *shit,*" he said, getting to his feet. He was neither surprised nor entirely angry. Part of taking on the role of full-time drug addict is a serious case of terminal resignation. It came with the territory.

Stepping out of the dingy restroom and into the afternoon sun was disconcerting. Timothy shielded his hypersensitive eyes from the glare with one hand and stroked his throbbing chin with the other. Blood oozed from an open gash. Timothy scanned the park, looking for someone he knew, someone he could trust. *Trust,* he thought. *That's laughable.*

Timothy still craved cocaine – powder, rock – it didn't matter. He just needed a fix. He wandered the park, scheming. He passed a group of heroin addicts sprawled under a tree in a quiet corner of the park. A few were passed out – on the nod – and the rest were openly injecting. They were a frightful group – gaunt, yellow-skinned, and dead-eyed. Those who were still conscious watched him pass with vacant expressions. They looked like the living dead, skeletal mannequins with leathery, human skin masks. They were creepy, even to Timothy. He walked by without a word.

Not far past the opiate users, clustered around a different tree, were the meth heads. Timothy knew a few of them, but generally avoided spending too much time in their company. They were a volatile, unpredictable bunch. He was recognized as he approached.

"Yo, Timmy!" yelled one of the tweakers. It was Sleaze, a rowdy but affable middle-aged user whom Timothy had met when he first started spending time with the other homeless people in the park. Sleaze had moved to the west from the east coast to work in the oil fields. He had developed a taste for amphetamines, as did many oil workers, which eventually led to him losing his job and entering the life of full-time addict.

"Hey, Sleaze," Timothy said. "How's it going, you crazy Newfie?"

"Brah, is *all* good," replied Sleaze. He had the typically thick, distinctive, and almost totally indecipherable accent of a Newfoundlander. "Wanna hit, brah? Come wit us – get *high*." Though nominally tempted, Timothy resisted. He preferred cocaine. Meth, and its users, scared him.

"Nah. Thanks, though." Timothy walked on, never slowing his pace.

"Nasty cut on yer chin dere, buddy!" Sleaze called out.

"Yup."

In the grimy underbelly of the city, finding people you can trust is difficult. Timothy's thoughts wandered to his old life of safety, success, and privilege. From the park, Timothy could clearly see the high-rises of downtown towering into the sky. He could even distinguish the buildings he once lived and worked in, so near...yet a virtual eternity away. He reflected on the life he once led and struggled to feel anything...except the inarticulate madness of the addict's appetite. "I need a hit," he muttered.

Evening had come. The sun was quickly setting. Timothy was getting increasingly desperate. It occurred to him that a meal would soon be served at a nearby soup kitchen. At that particular rescue mission, the food was generally quite good and the meals attracted a large portion of the city's homeless population. It was always a good place to mingle with the other inhabitants of the streets. Timothy wondered if he could perhaps score something there, even just a little bit to get him through the rest of the night.

Timothy walked two blocks to the mission in the peaceful twilight, his thoughts erratic and restless. There was an unpleasant, nauseous sensation swirling in his torso. He kept moving, pumping his legs mechanically. He hummed an indistinct tune in an effort to distract himself. It did not work very well.

Soon, he was in front of the rescue mission, the warm light of its interior spilling out onto the sidewalk and illuminating the ragtag mob of homeless, addicted, and mentally-ill people gathered outside. Timothy steeled himself as he merged with the crowd.

As he walked among them, Timothy surveyed the faces of the men and women who had congregated for the evening meal. An incredibly diverse group of people with disparate backgrounds and experiences frequented the mission, young and old, male and female, people of all races, temperament and demeanor, all with stories to tell, united by a shared history of hardship.

"Tim!" called a voice from the crowd. It was Keith, a regular at the mission and one of the first people Timothy had met when he began living on the streets. Keith was a 40-something hippy with a robust beard, long, matted hair, and a perpetual, goofy grin. He wore glasses with lens nearly an inch thick. His clothes were always filthy and he smoked pot constantly. Timothy could see him coming toward him now, leaning forward as he walked, eyes squinting, balled fists swinging at his side. He was a comical character, one of the few people Timothy trusted on the streets.

"Hey, buddy," Keith said. "Where ya been? Haven't seen you in a few days."

"Yeah, well...you know. Kinda got carried away with the..."

"Hittin' the pipe again, eh? That stuff is *nasty.* Look at

these people..." Keith gestured to the crowd gathered around them. "You want to be one of *them?* What a bunch of *bugs.*" He made no effort to lower his voice or hide his disdain.

"Stick with me," Keith said. "I've got it all figured out. I'm basically a dog, ya know? You can learn a lot from dogs. They don't need much to be happy, and neither do I. Give me a hole in the dirt to sleep in, some smoke, some scraps of food – that's all I need."

"Where have you been sleeping? Here, at the shelter?" Timothy asked.

"Fuck, no! Got a spot on the mountain," Keith replied. "Like I said, man, I'm a dog. I like sleeping outside in the open air. You should join me sometime. Once you learn to sleep outside you've got nothing left to fear, man."

Timothy nodded. "It's probably better than spending the night in this place." When he wasn't out all night chasing a high, Timothy had been sleeping on a cot in the mission for the last three months.

"The last night I spent in there was terrible," Timothy recalled. "The stench was *unbearable.* I never knew BO could be so bad until I slept in a shelter. Just a rancid, rotten smell. And the sounds! Ugh! All night – cough, cough, hack, hack...and the wet, repulsive snoring of a hundred sick and dirty men. Just horrible."

Keith laughed, a distinctive, high-pitched hyena's howl. "I know, buddy. How can you stand it?" Keith adjusted his glasses and squinted. He had once told Timothy that he was legally blind. The thick lenses distorted his eyes into exaggerated, bulging, bloodshot orbs. "Come to the hill with me tonight. I'll show you where I sleep."

Before Timothy could reply, a sudden, violent scuffle erupted beside them. Two men were swinging wildly at each other, both obviously highly intoxicated, their blows clumsy, inaccurate and awkward. Timothy and Keith took a few steps back to give the combatants a little space. The brawlers fell drunkenly on top of each other. A few more dispirited punches were exchanged while they lay on the sidewalk, then the fight was over. The crowd, who had watched the silly bout dispassionately, went back to whatever it was they were doing.

"As I was saying," Keith continued, "after dinner you should hike up the hill with me. I've got a great secluded spot overlooking the city."

Equilibrium was returning to Timothy's brain. The intense craving for cocaine was subsiding. The relief he felt was tempered by the knowledge that, soon enough, the desire to get high would no doubt return. It was a rhythmic thing, a waveform trick of the mind. Timothy had little control over where his thoughts went – but where his thoughts went, his body soon followed.

For now, though, he felt okay. It was good to just stand with Keith and the others and wait for a warm meal. An unexpected feeling of belonging warmed his heart. There was kinship here. Abandoned by their blood relatives, many street people found new families on the streets. With nowhere else to go and with no one else to trust, the homeless often found refuge and solace in shelters and rescue missions, taking comfort in the company of those who shared the experience of living on the streets.

A line was forming outside the mission, the patrons anticipating admittance. The regulars had done this countless times and organized themselves automatically, like nodes of a hive mind. Timothy and Keith fell into place.

"Smells like meatloaf," Timothy said.

"Smells like *ass*." Keith's face distorted in an exaggerated grimace.

The heavy door at the entrance to the mission opened.

The volunteer manning the door ushered people in. The line moved forward in a practiced, orderly fashion. Food was served in a cafeteria-style setting. Trays were provided at the counter. Volunteers scooped, scraped, and piled food cooked by other volunteers. The whole operation depended entirely on donations. Soup and sandwiches were standard lunch fare. The evening meal consisted of whatever was available in the pantry, but was generally warm and hearty. The entrée on this particular evening was, indeed, the much maligned meatloaf.

Timothy and Keith reached the counter and were served. They took their trays to a nearby table and sat in the first available seats. They were promptly joined by others. The table quickly filled.

"Busy tonight," Timothy observed.

"Getting close to the end of the month," Keith said. "Everyone spent their welfare checks on booze and drugs."

Keith, despite his proclamation concerning the smell of the food, immediately began shoveling meatloaf into his mouth. He ate in a manner similar to the way he lived – like a dog. He made loud grunting noises as he chewed. Chunks of food spilled out of his mouth and gathered in his tangled beard.

Timothy laughed. "Hungry, eh?" he said. Watching Keith eat was disgusting but somehow rather amusing. Keith ignored the comment and focused on delivering meatloaf from plate to mouth.

A man who had taken a seat across from them spoke: "Hey, you guys hear about Ol' Joe?"

Keith's curiosity was piqued. He stopped eating to catch up on the street gossip. "No," he said, "what about him?"

The other man, a regular at the mission, replied, "He OD'd last night. They found him lying in the grass at the park this morning, stiff and cold, with a needle still in his arm.

Poor guy."

Keith and Timothy had known Joe. He was a heroin addict who had been on the streets for years. He had been no older than they were, but looked positively ancient due to prolonged drug abuse.

"Bummer," Keith said. "I just talked to him last night. I *told* him the needle would get him! Damn." He turned to face Timothy, his face suddenly dead serious. "See," he said with intensity, "the hard stuff will kill you."

"HELL! THIS IS *HELL!!!*" A woman suddenly screamed at a table near the back wall. Everyone in the room turned to look as she stood up, threw her tray against the wall, and began clawing at her face. "Sick! Evil! Oh, no, God! HELP ME!!!" She was in serious mental distress. Her fingernails drew blood from her cheeks as she began weeping. Staff members moved in quickly in an attempt to restrain her.

"There she goes again," Keith said as he rolled his eyes. "Every night, like frickin' clockwork."

"Cops will be here soon," said the man who had informed the table of Ol' Joe's passing, "and I have warrants." He was up and out the door in a flash.

Keith went back to his meatloaf. Timothy was shaken. "I'm coming with you tonight," he said to Keith. "I need to get away from this place."

"Good!" Keith cried, meatloaf raining from his mouth.

When they finished eating, they went outside to have a cigarette. Timothy's thoughts once again turned to drugs. Keith, he knew, did not do cocaine. He smoked pot by the baleful, but avoided the 'hard stuff.' "That shit is for the *bugs*," he often cautioned Timothy. 'Bugs' was the term he used when referring to all the other street people. He had somehow developed a superiority complex.

Timothy and Keith puffed on their cigarettes and stood among the denizens of the street. The evening meal was over and the night was about to swallow them up in its secret, dangerous chambers. While mainstream society slept, madness, desperation, and depravity ruled the streets.

"There it is, buddy," said Keith, pointing to a small mountain in the distance. "That's mine. I marked it." To demonstrate exactly what he meant by 'marked,' Keith pantomimed urinating on the ground. "You're welcome to join me, though. My spot is secret, but I trust you."

There was truth in that statement. Somehow, despite his association with cocaine and its users, Timothy had gained Keith's trust. There was mutual admiration between the two. They had bonded instantly. Though from entirely different backgrounds, they had developed a strong friendship.

The impulse to stay on the streets and get high was strong, but Timothy felt the mountain calling him. It was a powerful draw – raw, primal magnetism.

"Let's do it," Timothy said.

The duo set out on their hike in the late evening hours. The mountains were ominous, imposing silhouettes on the horizon. A nearly-full moon hung in the sky, bathing the walkers in a cool, electric blue aura.

"It takes about an hour to get there," Keith said. "Hope that's okay with you."

"Whoa. I didn't realize it was so far."

"I like to keep my distance from the city at night. I feel safer up there, away from the bugs." Keith laughed his hyena cackle. "Sleeping on the street can get you robbed...or whacked. I'd rather take my chances with nature."

Timothy nodded. It made sense. His chin still ached from the assault he had suffered earlier in the day.

Timothy and Keith were walking through a residential neighborhood close to the city limits. The streets were eerily quiet. As they approached a large, rustic home on the corner, Keith pointed at the patio. "I got caught in the rain once on my way to the hill," he said. "I had to take cover under that patio, behind the firewood. I was just going to wait out the storm, but I got so comfortable I fell asleep and was there all night. I woke up in the morning to some guy kicking me in the side. 'Fuckin' bum!' he was yelling. I scrambled out of there pretty damn quick." Keith cackled again. He was enjoying the walk and the conversation.

"It's hard on the streets," Timothy said. "People just don't understand."

Keith took his glasses off and wiped them on his dirty sweater. Timothy could see just how visually impaired Keith was. His eyes had a cloudy, distant appearance.

"You know, I've been homeless for almost ten years now," Keith reflected. "One thing I've noticed is that people are, for the most part, good. The straight people, the junkies, the prostitutes, the crazies...everyone *wants* to be good, *wants* to be liked. We're all just doing the best we can given what we've got."

"I've met some truly nasty people, though," Timothy said. "Mean, cruel, vicious, *evil* people."

"Desperation brings out the best – and the worst – in us," Keith mused. "I've seen things on the street that would turn your stomach – brutal, destructive, yes, downright *evil* stuff...but I've also seen beauty, magic, real compassion and brotherhood. People on the streets take *care* of each other. There is genuine humanity on the streets."

They were nearing a gas station, beyond which lay only wilderness, foothills, and their destination, the small mountain Keith called home. "We should stop and get something to eat," Keith said. "Got any money?"

Timothy had a few dollars. It was money he had set aside for his habit, but the further they walked from the city, the less he craved the drug. "Yeah, a little," he said.

They entered the convenience store. The young man behind the counter looked up from his magazine, a scowl contorting his face. He said something under his breath, which sounded to Timothy suspiciously like, "Fuckin' bums." Keith had either not heard it or was unaffected by the insult. "Hey, buddy!" he called to the cashier with a smile and a wave.

"You really don't care what people think, do you?" Timothy said.

"Of course not!" Keith laughed. "Why would I? You can't please everyone." He gestured at the cashier and, without bothering to lower his voice, said, "Do you really think I care what a convenience store cashier thinks about me? Fuck, no!" The cashier's scowl deepened, but he remained silent and went back to his magazine.

Timothy admired Keith's total disregard for the opinions of other people. It was as if Keith had discovered the secret of true freedom – he had extricated himself from a mental prison. For Timothy, it was a revelation.

Timothy counted the change in his pocket. "I've got enough for some bread and bologna," he announced.

"Gourmet!" Keith exclaimed with real glee. Timothy gathered the items and approached the counter. The cashier completed the transaction without a word, contempt radiating from his reproachful eyes. Keith and Timothy left the store and resumed their walk.

"You never told me how you ended up on the streets," Timothy said. "I bet there's quite a story there."

Keith cackled. "Everyone's got a story. Mine is no more interesting than yours or anyone else's."

"I got hooked on coke. End of story."

"And yet here you are. Seems like your story isn't over."

"Fair enough, but I'm still curious – how did you end up homeless?" A moment of heavy silence followed. "If you don't want to tell me, that's cool."

"Want to know where I lived before I started living the dog's life?" Keith asked in a tone suddenly sincere and serious. "In a penitentiary, that's where. Five long years for a stupid mistake."

That surprised Timothy. Keith was slightly built and a little goofy-looking. He was streetwise and rough around the edges, but he had a kind soul. He did not seem to fit the profile of a hardened convict. Timothy considered asking him what crime he had committed, but decided against it. Keith would tell him when he was ready. This was the first time he had mentioned his incarceration – it seemed to be a sensitive subject.

"When I got out of prison," Keith said, "I simply couldn't handle being locked up anymore. I went from jail to a halfway house and I just couldn't take it. From one cell to another, basically. I hated it. I tried getting my own apartment but that didn't work. It was hard for me to even be indoors. One night, I slept in the woods – I liked it."

"A dog's life, right?"

"You got that right, buddy. Been living that way ever since...going on ten years. I moved to BC because the weather's nicer. I can stay on the mountain almost all year round."

They were nearing the path that would take them up the hill to Keith's camp. The trail started at the end of a residential street and took them into a provincial park. The park was closed to the public at night and camping was strictly prohibited, but Keith's spot was well hidden and he was always careful to avoid being seen by the rangers who made occasional patrols.

"Here we go, buddy," Keith said. They were at the trailhead. The hill loomed in the dark directly ahead, intimidating and menacing. "This trail will take us most of the way and then we have to do a little bushwhacking."

"Fair enough," Timothy said. Night hiking made him a little nervous, but the excitement of embarking on a grand adventure was fortifying.

"Watch for snakes," Keith said casually, "and try to stay quiet, at least until we get off the trail. We don't want to attract any attention."

They hiked in silence, penetrating the darkness. Keith led and Timothy followed directly behind. The densely-forested hill embraced them in velvety shades of dark blue. A gentle breeze rustled branches and swept across the two hikers. Timothy began to experience an exquisite sensation – he felt real, he felt free, he felt far from the anxiety and meaningless ennui of society. The feeling was better than any drug he had ever tried. It was as if he, too, had been released from mental captivity.

They began to ascend as the trail led them up the hill. Keith and Timothy hiked on, each content to silently explore his own thoughts. Timothy's mind traveled to his life before the streets, to his life as an advertising executive – eons ago, seemingly. What a strange trajectory he had been on – a bizarre set of events had taken him from the pinnacle of so-called success to this moment now, sneaking up a mountain at night with a homeless man. Oddly, for the first time since his early childhood, Timothy felt entirely at peace.

Keith suddenly stopped in front of him. "Over there," he whispered. "Check it out." Timothy looked in the direction Keith was indicating...and was stunned. There, lurking in the dark mere feet from their location on the trail, stood a large elk, its antlers clearly visible in stark silhouette. Moonlight was reflected in its huge, deep eyes. The elk simply stood there, watching the two humans.

"Wow!"

"Amazing, eh?" Keith said in a low voice. "I see 'em all the time. They won't hurt you." Timothy took Keith's word for it and the two continued their hike. The elk observed their passing with solemn ambivalence.

"Here's where we take the road less traveled," Keith said not far from where they had seen the elk. He broke from the trail and began pushing through the underbrush. "It gets a little tricky here," he said. "Might have to use your hands."

The ascent became noticeably steeper and Timothy did indeed need to use his hands as he climbed. It was rocky and tangled, difficult to traverse. The darkness made it hard for Timothy to know exactly where to place his hands. Ahead of him, Keith scrambled expertly, making quick progress. Timothy lost sight of him. Just as fear began to set in, he heard Keith call from above:

"Here we are, buddy! You made it!"

After climbing a few more feet Timothy reached the plateau on which Keith was perched. Keith extended a hand and helped him with the final steps. Timothy sat beside Keith on a patch of ground beneath a massive Douglas fir. They were overlooking the city and the view was stunning – so unexpectedly, breathtakingly gorgeous that Timothy actually gasped.

"Nice, eh?" Keith cackled. "I told you."

Below, the lights of the city sparkled like a field of stars spread out upon the earth, twinkling orange, blue, red, and white. Timothy felt absolutely fantastic, like a conquering god perched upon his throne.

"Here's where I live," Keith said. "This is where I

belong."

Timothy spent a few minutes soaking up the view and then turned his attention to the camp that Keith had created on the hillside. It was little more than a small clearing in the dirt. There was no real sign of human habitation.

"I've got some sleeping bags, blankets, and pillows for us," Keith said. He got up and retrieved a large garbage bag stuffed with bedding that he had hidden in the bushes earlier that day. "Gotta keep this stuff wrapped up."

Keith spread out the sleeping bags and blankets in the clearing and then reclined on the bed he had made, his head propped up on a pillow. "Get comfortable," he urged Timothy.

Timothy made himself comfortable. "Oh, yeah," he said. "This is actually pretty nice!" It had been a long, eventful day, and the hike from the city and up the hill had been strenuous. It felt good to be lying there in the fresh air, under the stars, with the gentle sounds of the night forest drifting by on the breeze.

"This is amazing," Timothy said. "Simplicity, beauty...what a life." He looked over at Keith and was amused to see that his companion had already fallen asleep. Keith's glasses lay on the ground beside him. His mouth was agape. A rhythmic snore rose from his throat. He had the look of a man with a crystal clear conscience. Timothy smiled.

Sleep took Timothy not long after. He slumbered in peaceful repose, cradled in his nest on the mountain. Hours passed. Nature went about its nocturnal business as the two men slept.

Sometime in the middle of the night, Timothy awoke with a start. Confusion reigned for a few moments as he struggled to recall exactly where and who he was. He regained his grasp on reality with relief. He was on a mountain. His friend Keith was asleep beside him. It was good.

Still, something was not quite right. A light...a strange light now surrounded him. Where was it coming from? It was white and growing in intensity. It appeared to be shining down from above like a giant spotlight in the sky. Timothy had to shield his eyes from the intense glare. The forest was now brightly illuminated. Timothy could see animals, large and small, scurrying between the trees in a panic. The unnaturally powerful light was moving now, casting ghostly, elongated shadows. Timothy looked over at Keith, who was still fast asleep, snoring and drooling, completely unaware of the weird event unfolding.

Timothy sat up and instinctively wrapped a blanket around his trembling shoulders. The source of the light was now directly over him. It was obviously artificial and emanated from an incredibly immense airborne object that was passing silently over the mountain. The object was so large that it blacked out all of the stars in the sky above the valley. It appeared to be a mile long and a mile wide. The outline was vaguely triangular, but from Timothy's vantage point, it was impossible to distinguish its true shape.

The craft stopped moving. It hung above the two men on the mountain, its brilliant light trained on their position. Timothy was frozen in abject fear – and awe. His mind went blank. He could neither comprehend nor process what he was seeing. An electrical crackling sound from the craft broke the silence. A light *within* the light appeared, a pale blue beam, which moved as if it were composed of solid particles. It descended down the luminous white glow. It reached Timothy. Timothy could actually feel the beam as it embraced him. Serenity, warm and luxurious – Timothy drifted, or was guided, back to sleep.

In the morning, the memory of what Timothy had

witnessed was vivid, the vision of the craft moving over the valley indelibly stamped on his mind. It had not been a dream, he was certain of that. The soft light of early day filled the misty valley and warmed the mountain. Timothy shook off the remnants of sleep and sat admiring the view.

Keith, he realized, had disappeared. Timothy's imagination ran through a series of supernatural scenarios to account for Keith's absence. He could visualize him spread-eagle on an alien examination table while bulbous-headed, gray creatures poked and prodded him with bizarre implements...

"Good morning!" It was Keith. He was emerging from the bushes to Timothy's left. "Nothing like a good piss to start the day!" he announced cheerfully. "Especially when it's in the great outdoors, eh?" Keith cackled.

"Whew, I thought you were...gone," Timothy said, relieved. He pondered how to broach the subject of the night's weird events. "So...last night," he finally chose to say. "Did you sleep well?"

"Of course I did. I always sleep well. What about you, buddy?"

"You didn't see anything *unusual?*" Timothy prodded.

"Like a UFO?" Keith said flatly. "Not last night, no. Seen 'em before, though. They usually come out after I've already crashed for the night. Why, did you see one?"

Keith's response caught Timothy off guard. It was not the answer he had expected. "Yes," he said. "I think I saw a UFO."

"Yeah, they're common around here. When I first started sleeping on the hill I used to see them every night. It was exciting...at first. The novelty wears off pretty quick." Keith produced two bent cigarettes from a crumpled pack, offering one to Timothy and lighting the other for himself.

Timothy puffed in silence while he considered what

Keith had just revealed. Oddly, he did not experience any serious cognitive incongruities. His mind assimilated the information with no real difficulty.

"Interesting," Timothy said. "That's very interesting."

"We live in a different world, buddy." Keith slapped Timothy on the back. "When you're living on the streets you get to see some pretty weird shit."

The two men sat on the mountain and smoked their cigarettes. In the valley below, people were getting up and preparing for the day – showers and toothbrushes, breakfast and small talk, newspapers and daily commutes. The masses lived their quiet lives of quotidian banality, completely oblivious to the secrets of a world lying parallel to their own.

The Ward

At the age of 30, Samuel lost his will to live. It was not sudden, but rather a slow and steady process of mental and emotional deterioration, culminating in a state of total, abject despair. Samuel had always been moody and prone to bouts of depression, but the internal desolation that overcame him as an adult was despondency of the highest order.

One day, Samuel woke up and thought, *Today is the day I will kill myself.* It was a pure, crystalline idea – the clear and final solution. After years of turmoil he could finally see a way out. The problem of his existence had been solved and the answer was to cease to exist.

For Samuel, suicide had become something much larger than the negation of his life. The concept itself fascinated him. Contemplating its immense profundity excited him. He fantasized about the various ways that he could exit this world with style. Samuel wanted his death to make a statement in a way his life had not.

Samuel was an artist. He painted in an abstract Expressionist fashion with vibrant and energetic colors on large canvasses. The peak of his depression coincided with a period of creative frustration. While staring at a blank and mocking canvas, a delicious idea occurred to him: *I will make my final act a literal work of art.*

It was a wonderfully creative idea for a burned out, suicidal artist: Get a gun, sit in front of a large canvas, and blow off your own head, splattering blood and brain tissue onto the white surface. To Samuel, it seemed brilliant – a perfect way to end both his emotional anguish and his artistic block. It would be the ultimate mode of self-expression...it might even make him posthumously famous.

Samuel spent a few days preparing for his departure, obtaining the materials he required, including a pistol procured from a pawn shop. During the planning and logistics phase of his project, he experienced a surprising sensation of elation. Soon, he knew, his mind and its troublesome thoughts – and his heart, with its inconvenient sensitivities – would dissipate, evaporate, and dissolve into blissful nothingness. This knowledge filled him with peace. He felt better than he had in a decade.

On the morning of his planned suicide, Samuel loaded and cocked his gun and stood in front of a blank canvas which he had arranged and secured to a wall in his apartment. He had not written a note. His final 'painting' would suffice. He took a deep breath and put the gun in his mouth. He closed his eyes. His thoughts wandered into strange corridors. In his mind's eye, he saw flashes of old friends, glimpses of distant family, and random, disjointed scenes from his short life. The memories filled him with melancholy and longing. Tears welled in Samuel's eyes. His finger closed on the trigger of the gun.

A sudden, forceful knock at his apartment door shattered the moment. "Sam, you in there?" called a voice from the hall. It was his neighbor Nick.

"Sam, I need to talk to you," Nick insisted. "It's important!" *Everything* was important to Nick. He lived in perpetual crisis mode. He was nosy, bothersome, and dramatic, but he was also loyal, dependable, and kind. Samuel considered him to be one of his few true friends.

Samuel removed the gun from his mouth and sighed. "Give me a minute, Nick," he said. Samuel hastily hid the gun under some papers on an end table and went to the door. He opened the door and there stood Nick with a comically exaggerated look of distress on his face. Typical.

Nick immediately began spewing words. "Cathy has

totally lost it," he said, referring to a tenant of the apartment building who lived on the floor above them. "I can't *take* it any more. She's driving me *crazy.*" Without waiting to be invited in, Nick walked right past Samuel and into the apartment. He sat on the couch and continued his diatribe.

"She came down this morning to ask for some milk for her coffee," Nick said, entirely oblivious to the scene he had just walked in on...and unaware that he had just interrupted a suicide attempt. Samuel groaned internally and prepared for the long haul. Nick's stories had a tendency to ramble on and on and *on...*

"So I *give* her the damn milk, okay?" Nick continued. "And guess what? She's back down ten minutes later. 'Got any bread? Got any cheese?' God! She's so *annoying!*"

"Yeah, I know what you mean."

"Have you seen her today?"

"No, I..." Samuel paused. "I've been busy this morning."

Nick nodded at the blank canvas hanging on the wall. "Painting?" he asked. In that moment, Samuel seriously considering telling Nick everything that he had thought, felt, and done over the past few days as he moved seemingly inexorably toward a tragic death at his own hands. *Talk to him,* he thought. *Talk to someone. It would be good.* He chose, instead, to keep the gritty details to himself. "I haven't been feeling too hot," he said.

Nick's expression showed genuine concern. "How so? Want to talk about it?"

"Now's probably not a good time. I didn't sleep well last night. I think I just need to be alone for a bit. Rest, maybe eat. Thanks, though."

Nick uncharacteristically took the hint. "Well, then," he said as he rose from the couch, "I guess I should take off. Feel free to come over later and talk. I'm here for you, man."

Nick's sincerity was touching. "I appreciate that, Nick," Samuel said. "I'll try to pop by later."

"Okay, man. See ya." Nick left the apartment. Samuel closed the door behind him and simply stood there, his emotions complex. He cast a glace toward the gun beneath the paper on the table. His enthusiasm for a quick and violent end had diminished.

Samuel felt a surge of unpleasant feelings – embarrassment, guilt, fear...but mostly a great sadness, as if he had peered into the deepest recesses of his soul and discovered it to be lacking. *I'm a coward,* he thought. He wanted nothing more than to climb into bed and slide into a dreamless sleep for the rest of eternity.

He made it to bed before succumbing to uncontrollable heavy weeping. He lay there and cried, frustration and sorrow welling up from a bottomless pit within his defeated heart. Spent, he slid into unconsciousness and slept for 12 hours.

In the middle of the night, Samuel awoke, sweaty, hungry, weak, and alone. It was shocking for him to realize just how close he had been, only hours before, to putting a bullet in his head. Visualizing the event now filled him with existential horror. His soul shuddered.

Samuel got out of bed. In his empty apartment he felt more isolated and depressed than ever. The strange thing was, he could not identify the real source of his depression. Where and when had it started? It was as if a dark force had infiltrated his life at some unknown point in the past, and it now had total control over his thoughts and emotions. Subversive and invasive, the malignant influence had crept in and rooted itself in his mind. After years of psychic corrosion, Samuel had been left powerless and hopeless.

I wonder if Nick is awake, Samuel thought. In his

weakened, vulnerable state, Samuel was able to recognize his need to interact with another person. He yearned to unload some of the mental burden he had acquired. He longed to release the pressure that had built in his overworked mind. Conversation would be good.

Samuel climbed out of bed and left his apartment. The halls were quiet and empty in the middle of the night. He roamed the apartment building like a restless ghost. He arrived at Nick's door and knocked quietly. No answer. He waited for a few minutes before trying again, this time a little more forcefully. Again, no reply. Samuel thought he heard movement in the apartment.

"Nick," he said in a loud whisper. "It's Sam. You up? I need to talk to you."

More movement and rustling from within. "Okay, okay...one sec," Nick said in a strained, distant voice. Faint cursing and strange clanging sounds followed. Samuel dared not speculate on what weird activities Nick might have been up to in the middle of the night.

The deadbolt was released, the door opened, and there stood Nick, disheveled and out of breath. "Hey, buddy," he said. "What's up?"

"Just wondering what was going on with you. I couldn't sleep. Thought maybe you might wanna stop by for a chat."

"Uh...sure." Nick glanced back into his apartment. "How about I stop by in a few minutes? I just need to...clean up."

"No problem."

Samuel returned to his apartment, and in a few minutes, heard a knock at his door.

"You look rough," Nick said to Samuel as he entered Samuel's apartment.

"I know it," Samuel admitted. Nick took a seat beside

him on the couch and lit a cigarette.

"Care to talk about it?" Nick asked. Samuel had hoped to do exactly that, but found it difficult to start. He hesitated, rubbing a spot on his forehead just above his left eye. Honesty, blunt and direct, seemed like the best approach.

"I planned to kill myself today," Samuel said. "Obviously, it didn't work out."

Nick froze mid-puff, clearly shocked. "*What? Seriously? Shit, man. I didn't know. You should have talked to me earlier.*"

"Who knows what would have happened if you hadn't interrupted. I'm glad you did, though, because I changed my mind."

Nick was disturbed. "That's some heavy shit, man," he said. "You should talk to somebody."

"I *am*," Samuel said.

"I mean a professional. I'm here for you, buddy, but there are people out there who could *really* help you...doctors, psychiatrists...*professionals.* They got some good drugs now, you know. I've been on medication for almost my whole life. Couldn't imagine living without it. I'd be a mess."

Nick finished his cigarette and stubbed it out in an ashtray on the coffee table. He was a heavy smoker. Samuel could see dark, ugly yellow stains on his index and middle fingers. Nick was a weird dude and Samuel was not surprised to find out that he was on medication. He could only speculate on how weird he'd be *off* the pills.

"You're a good guy, Sam," Nick said as he rose from the couch and headed for the door. "Don't let the world get you down. I have an early appointment, so I gotta get some sleep, but I'm here for you, buddy. Any time you wanna talk, let me know...and consider what I said about seeing a professional. It worked for me."

"Will do. Thanks for stopping by."

Nick slipped out the door. Samuel sat once again in solitary silence. Before he had a chance to reign them in, his thoughts wandered to the gun he had stashed under his papers on the end table. It was within arms reach. Samuel's rampant imagination displayed a graphic scene in his mind's eye – an explosion of skull, skin, hair, and brain. He was losing control over his mental space. His thoughts were betraying him.

Disturbed, Samuel attempted to shake off the violent, suicidal ideation. He paced the apartment. He played music. He wandered into the kitchen for a snack. The visions returned – persistent, relentless, taunting. *Kill yourself,* a low, maniacal voice inside him insisted. *Do it. Do it NOW. It's easy, instant, painless.* Gory images of self-destruction looped in his head.

Samuel's survival instinct, primal and powerful, engaged. His psyche had fractured into two opposing factions, one driving toward total destruction, one fighting desperately for his continued existence. In the wrestling match for his soul, Samuel's lust for the void submitted to his desire for life. He picked up a telephone and made a call.

"911, what is your emergency?"

"I need help. I'm suicidal."

Samuel was taken by ambulance to the regional hospital. His speech and behavior prompted the medical technicians to inject him with a sedative. Strangely, the first real treatment he received for his depression was the administration of a central nervous system depressant. The effect was instantly calming. Samuel arrived at the hospital and was brought to the emergency ward for processing.

After a brief interview in triage, Samuel was escorted to a tiny waiting room with an examination table. He was given a hospital gown. He stripped, put on the gown, and sat on the table. An overweight nurse with malice in her eyes entered the room and slipped on a pair of rubber gloves. "I need to take your vitals," she said, yawning as she spoke.

"Okay," Samuel said.

The nurse's plump hands explored Samuel's body. Vital signs were taken.

"Am I alive?" Samuel joked.

"Yes," the nurse answered as she removed the gloves and disposed of them. She exited the room without another word, leaving Sam on the examination table. He felt vulnerable and violated. All he could do was wait, so he did.

Hours passed. Samuel shifted his position on the table and drifted in and out of consciousness. Sounds from the emergency ward carried through the walls. It was a busy night at the hospital. While Samuel oscillated between sleep and wakefulness, strange audio penetrated the walls of the small room – moans, screams of agony, demented shouts of the senile and desperate. Someone begged for pain killers, another hurled a barrage of obscenities at hospital staff members. It was a long, weird night.

In the early morning, a professionally dressed young woman entered the room. Samuel had been lying on the table in a state of near awareness for many hours. He heard her come in.

"Hello," the woman said in a pleasant voice. "I'm Dr. Philips. May I ask you a few questions?"

"Yes, of course." Samuel was extremely relieved to have the opportunity to talk to someone.

The doctor sat in a seat next to the table. She consulted a clipboard she had brought in with her. "Samuel," she said. "Or do you prefer Sam?"

"Sam is fine."

"Sam, would you like to tell me what brought you in?"

"Whew, that's a tough question. I guess the simple answer is that I've been...depressed."

Dr. Philips began taking notes. "How long have you been feeling this way?"

Samuel began to feel self-conscious. Sharing the details of his private, internal struggle with a total stranger was going to be much harder than he had anticipated. *Have I made a colossal mistake?* he thought. As if in response, a technicolor vision of violent suicide flashed in his mind. He shook it off and attempted to articulate the mental distress he had been experiencing.

Dr. Philips could sense his reticence to share. "I'm not here to judge you," she said. "I'm here to help you. Any information you can provide will help me determine the best possible course of treatment."

"Well," Samuel said, gathering the courage to expose the inner workings of his mind. "I'm here because I'm seriously considering killing myself. It's an idea I've long been fascinated with, but lately I've been obsessed. I guess I'm talking to you now because, somewhere deep inside, I really don't want to die."

Dr. Philips looked Samuel in the eye and smiled. "Good," she said. "That's a start, isn't it?"

The conversation continued for close to an hour, mostly covering Samuel's and his family's histories of mental illness and emotional aberrations, but also meandering into seemingly irrelevant directions. Samuel spilled his guts. He purged himself of years of pent-up frustration and turmoil. The relief he felt as the pressure was released was near orgasmic. Dr. Philips took extensive notes.

At the end of the interview, Dr. Philips said, "I think it would be best for you to be admitted to the hospital as an in-patient. How do you feel about that, Sam?"

"I'm officially crazy," Samuel deadpanned. "Certifiably, undeniably *nuts*. It's not as painful as I thought it would be..."

"We don't use terms like that here, Sam, and even if we did, I wouldn't necessarily apply them to you. You *are* depressed, though. That much is obvious. With the right treatment, including medication and counseling, I think you could lead a very normal and fulfilling life."

"I'm not sure if I'll ever be *normal*, but fulfilled, or at least somewhat happy, would be nice."

With a few strokes of the doctor's pen, Samuel became a psychiatric patient. Being admitted to the ward was like gaining admission to an underground world, a secret realm with its own codes, customs, and hierarchies – a bizarre tangential universe filled with misfits and maniacs.

A nurse escorted Samuel from the emergency room to the psychiatric ward. Despite being able-bodied and relatively physically fit he was transported in a wheelchair. He voiced his objections and was told that it was simply a matter of hospital protocol. The wheelchair made him feel much more ill than he was. It set a disturbing precedent.

Samuel was wheeled up to the main nurse's desk. Introductions were made and paperwork was exchanged. The head nurse at reception was a kind, middle-aged woman with a gentle, patient demeanor.

"Would you like me to take you to your bed, Sam?" the head nurse asked. She spoke to Samuel as if he were a child...or as if he had a psyche as fragile as frosted glass.

"Sure," Samuel replied.

The nurse's desk sat at the center of an intersection of hallways. The nurse led Samuel down one of the brightly-lit, eggshell white halls. It was late afternoon and very quiet on the ward. The doors to most of the rooms were closed. Samuel could hear faint conversation, snoring, and even soft sobbing coming from the unseen occupants. The nurse stopped at the last door on the left. "This is your room," she said.

Samuel stepped into the room. There were two beds separated by a curtain which was currently drawn. Samuel could see the silhouette of his roommate on the far bed near the window. The nurse gestured at the bed closest to the door and said, "This is your bed."

"Are those your street clothes?" the nurse asked, referring to a large bag Samuel was carrying. He had been given the bag while in the emergency ward. It contained all of the personal items he had brought with him to the hospital.

"Yes, among other things."

"For your safety – and the safety of the other patients, I'll need to screen your belongings."

"Can I change back into my clothes?" Samuel was still wearing the flimsy hospital gown, which made him feel self-conscious.

"In time, yes. That is usually at the doctor's discretion. For the first few days, patients are advised to wear gowns."

"Okay." Samuel was feeling a little like an inmate already. He emptied the bag onto the bed. It didn't contain much, just the clothes he had been wearing when he arrived, his keys, and his wallet.

"Did you bring any personal hygiene products?" the nurse asked.

"No, I did not. Wasn't sure how long I'd be here or if I'd need anything like that."

"That's okay. We can provide you with soap, shampoo, a toothbrush, and toothpaste. Razors are provided upon doctor's approval. Do you have any sharp items? Pen, pocketknife, pins?"

"Nope. If I really wanted to hurt myself, I'd have done it already. Ha."

The nurse was not amused. "My concern is for the safety of *all* patients," she said. "Do you wear a belt? If so, I'll need to take that as well." The question filled Samuel's head with grim images of patients hanging from the hospital rafters. "No," he said.

"Okay. If you could please bag up your belongings, we will store them until you are cleared to wear street clothes."

Samuel did so. The nurse took the bag and said, "if you'd like to come with me, I can show you around the ward." Samuel followed her out the door and back into the hall.

The first stop was the TV room. "This is where most patients choose to spend their time," the nurse said. The room was full of drugged and docile patients staring blankly at an inane music video. It was a spooky scene.

The nurse led Samuel down another hall, stopping in front of a large, empty dining room. "This is where meals are served," she said. "Dinner will be served very soon, at 4:30. Breakfast is at 7 AM, lunch at 11:30."

They moved on. "Here is the recreation room," the nurse said, stopping at a room with a bookshelf, couches, and a mini grand piano. Two elderly women were playing a silent game of chess. They looked up in unison at Samuel and the nurse.

"This is Sam," the nurse said. "Sam, this is Margaret and Lucy. Feel free to come here to relax, read, or play a game any time you aren't seeing your doctor or participating in a group session."

"Fresh meat! How sweet!" A voice reverberated down the hall. A young man was skipping toward Samuel and the nurse like a child playing a game of hopscotch. His hair was a shaggy brown rat's nest. Instead of a hospital gown he wore Teenage Mutant Ninja Turtle pajamas.

"Hello, Graham," the nurse said as the young man approached. "We have a new patient on the ward. His name is Sam."

"Sam, Sam, Sam...wham, bam, thank you ma'am!" Graham sang. Samuel was surprised to see that, upon closer inspection, Graham appeared to be in his late teens or early twenties – his infantile behavior could not hide the fact that he was in serious need of a shave.

"Hi," Samuel said.

"Hi!" Graham waved like a toddler. "Wanna play Transformers?"

"Maybe later, Graham. Let Sam settle in first, okay?" The nurse spoke to Graham patiently and with kindness. An exaggerated pout appeared on Graham's face. He began chewing on his fingernails. "Awww," he moaned, "you're mean."

"I'll play later," Samuel said. "I like Transformers." Graham immediately cheered up. "Sam, Sam, Sam...wham, bam, thank you ma'am!" he cried joyously as he skipped away down the hall.

"Graham has been with us for a while," the nurse said. "He can be a challenge, but he's a good...kid."

The nurse checked her watch. "That concludes the basic tour," she said. "Dinner will be served shortly. If you have any questions, I'd be happy to answer them."

"When does my treatment begin?" Samuel asked. "When will I see the doctor again?"

"There will be a team meeting in the morning – psychiatrists, psychologists, nurses, and social workers. The team will establish the best course of treatment based on your individual needs. I expect that you will meet with a doctor sometime after that. In the meantime, make yourself comfortable. Feel free to stay in your room or explore the ward, but you will need doctor's approval to leave this floor. If medication has been prescribed, you will receive it at mealtimes and before bed."

It was a lot to process. Samuel was beginning to feel more like a prisoner than a patient. He did feel safe, however. It was good to be somewhere other than his apartment, given the dark and disturbed thoughts rattling around in his head.

"Thank you," Samuel said. "If it's okay, I think I'll just rest in my room for now."

"That's an excellent idea," the nurse said. "If you need anything, just ask me or one of the other nurses at the desk." She gave Samuel a genuinely warm smile and returned to her post.

Samuel made his way back to his room. The curtain between his bed and his roommate's was still pulled across the space, the silhouette of the individual on the bed still visible. Samuel climbed onto his bed. Reclining, he folded his hands over his chest and closed his eyes. He attempted to clear his mind.

Samuel's thoughts wandered, retracing the series of events that had brought him from the brink of total collapse to this strange, new environment, from a close call with death by self-inflicted gunshot to a bed in a psychiatric ward. He wondered about the other patients of the institution – the stories, the pain, the tragedy, the madness...

"What are you in for?" called a voice from the other bed. It was his new roommate. An arm appeared and drew back the curtain. Samuel got his first look at the mysterious individual on the other side – a thin, bespectacled man with a shaven head. It took a moment for Samuel to realize that the man had also shaved off his eyebrows.

"Pardon me?" Samuel asked, slightly shocked at the man's appearance.

"What are you in for?" the man repeated. "Depression? Drugs? General insanity?"

"Oh..." Samuel hesitated. "Um...depression, I guess."

"Exactly what I thought!" the man said. "I can always tell." The man was clearly pleased with himself. "Suicidal?" he asked. The tone in his voice was casual. He could have been asking Samuel about his favorite sports team.

"I thought so, but I'm not so sure now," Samuel replied. "I guess if I really wanted to kill myself, I would have."

"Interesting," the man said, obviously not interested at all in Samuel's philosophical musings. "How were you going to do it? Pills? Rope? Gun? I cut my wrists, see?" The man displayed his wrists for Samuel. Both were wrapped in thick layers of gauze. "Did one and then, while it was gushing blood, used that hand to do the other. What a *mess!*" The man laughed. He was proud of his deed and enjoyed telling the story.

"Yikes."

"The doctors said they were the deepest cuts they had seen in a long time. I think they were really impressed!" The man stood up and extended his hand in greeting. "I'm Trevor, but my friends call me T-bone."

Samuel shook Trevor's hand very carefully, conscious of the wound on his wrist. He allowed his morbid imagination a moment to visualize the damage before introducing himself.

"I'm Sam."

"It's nice to meet you, Sam. You'll like it here."

"Nice to meet you, too."

Samuel returned to a reclined position. Trevor sat on the edge of his own bed.

"It's my family that did it. They drove me crazy."
Trevor launched into his life story, oblivious to Samuel's
reluctance to engage in deep conversation. "Parents divorced
when I was two years old. Lived with mom after that, and she
drank like a damn fish. Know what I mean?"

"I think so..."

"She always had these awful, abusive men around,"
Trevor continued. "Got the shit kicked out of me constantly.
Really fucks ya up, y'know?"

"Listen, Trevor..."

"T-bone. Friends call me T-bone."

"Listen, T-bone, I'm really not feeling well. If you
don't mind, I'm just going to lie here for a bit and try to nap."

"Don't want to miss dinner, do you?" Trevor's ability
to pick up on social cues was severely lacking. "Gonna be
served soon. You gotta eat."

"Yes, I know." Samuel was exasperated. "I just need a
few minutes. It's been a long day. I am *really* tired."

"Oh, I understand!" Trevor exclaimed, sensing an
opportunity to fill the air with his voice again. "My first day
here was *brutal!* And don't forget, I was seriously injured!
You should have seen the slices on my wrists...cut clear to
the *bone...*"

Samuel closed his eyes. Trevor finally got the hint.
"You should get some sleep, Sam." he said. "You'll definitely
need your rest. This place will drive you crazy if you weren't
already! Hahaha!"

"Of that I have no doubt," Samuel said. Trevor kept
speaking, but Samuel was very effective in his attempts to
filter out the sound of the voice. Trevor's rambling speech
faded...faded...until Samuel found a quiet mental space in
which to linger. He lay there, peacefully suspended in the
timeless place between sleep and wakefulness.

Just as Samuel was slipping into deep sleep, a shrill

voice shattered his repose. "Time to *eat!*" shrieked Trevor in pure delight as he bounded by Samuel's bed and out the door. Dinner was being served in the dining room. Samuel was groggy, but hungry. He slid out of bed and shambled down the hall.

The ward was now a bustling hive of activity. Patients of both genders in a wide variety of ages and states of awareness were moving through the halls and congregating in the dining room. Samuel moved among them, feeling like a refugee from a distant land called Sanity.

Inside the dining room, food trays were already in place. Samuel approached the nearest tray and, and as he was about to seat himself in front of it, a woman with wild hair and vacant eyes pushed him out of the way. "Mine," she said.

Trevor was already seated and eating. He spotted Samuel. "Look for a tray with your name on it," he said. The other patients, who were already familiar with the meal time protocol, were quickly finding their assigned meals and settling into place. Samuel began examining the unclaimed trays and, sure enough, he found one with his name on it.

Samuel sat down...and found himself facing a person wearing a rubber mask of Freddy Krueger, the supernatural villain from *A Nightmare on Elm Street*. The robust build and hairy hands of the individual indicated a male. The man was attempting to eat, spooning soup through the mouth hole. Some of the soup seemed to be reaching his mouth, but most of it was slopping and splattering down on to his hospital gown and the table. The man was staring directly at Samuel, his foggy, bloodshot eyes visible behind the mask.

"Hi, Freddy," Samuel said. The man offered no reply. Warm, chunky soup dripped from the rubber chin.

Seated beside Samuel was a young, petite, dark-haired girl. She was crouched over her food in a defensive posture, her right arm curled around the tray as if she were eating in a prison cafeteria. Samuel realized that she was weeping as she ate. Tears were raining down upon her food as she cried uncontrollably. She swallowed between bouts of violent shaking.

"Is everything okay?" Samuel was truly concerned. The young girl continued to sob as she ate, inconsolable and unreachable. The man in the Freddy Krueger mask decided to speak. "She never talks," he said. "She just cries all day...*every* day."

Compassion and empathy stirred within Samuel's heart. For a moment, at least, his own troubles seemed trivial. He pondered what profound distress, what psychic horror, the young lady seated beside him must have been experiencing. Samuel felt genuine sympathy for her and, at the same time, though he was mostly unaware of it, his own healing had begun. *I wish I could help you,* he thought. *I wish I could at least ease your pain.*

A very strange thing happened. Just as Samuel's thoughts turned to the young woman and his desire to alleviate her suffering, her weeping ceased. She looked up from her meal and said, in a voice barely above a whisper, "It's okay." The woman's mouth formed an almost imperceptible smile, and then the tears began to flow again as she returned to her meal. It was a surreal moment.

Samuel went with the flow. He removed the plastic lid from his tray, exposing a decent enough looking meal of sliced turkey and vegetables. He began to eat, and was relieved to discover that the food was more than palatable. It was, in fact, quite tasty.

Samuel dined on hospital food, surrounded by psychiatric patients with a vast spectrum of disorders and conditions. The collection of unusual minds gathered in the room formed a matrix, a mosaic, a tangibly skewed tapestry of strange proportions and oblique dimensions. Samuel felt like a node in a giant, diseased hive mind. Trevor's words returned to him: *This place will drive you crazy if you weren't already!*

A nurse was making rounds in the dining room, delivering medication to each patient. She reached Samuel and stopped. She examined the labels on the tiny cups she carried on a tray. Each cup contained an assortment of pills in a variety of sizes and colors. "I have your meds, Sam," she said, offering him a cup. Samuel was surprised that the doctor had acquired enough information in their first, brief session together to make an accurate diagnosis.

"What *are* those?" Samuel asked, peering into the cup. The nurse also carried a clipboard. She checked the attached paperwork. "The doctor has prescribed Effexor, an antidepressant, lithium carbonate, a mood stabilizer, and clonazepam for anxiety and to help with sleep. You will receive the Effexor and lithium now, and the clonazepam before bed."

"Wow," Samuel said. "That seems like a lot of drugs."

"That's a fairly typical regimen," the nurse said.

"Do I *have* to take the pills?"

The nurse gave Samuel a stern look. "To refuse your medication would be to go against the doctor's orders and that may jeopardize your future treatment. I recommend you take the pills now and discuss your concerns with the doctor when you see her next."

The nurse was persuasive. Samuel took the cup and washed the pills down with a gulp of water. "Good," the nurse said, and moved on to the next person. The other patients took their medication with no objections. Some had been eagerly anticipating pill time and gobbled up their meds with glee.

Samuel finished his meal. He observed other patients placing their empty trays on a large, rolling, multilevel cart. He followed their lead and then wandered back out into the hall. Trevor approached. "Nasty meal, eh?" he exclaimed, slapping Samuel on the back playfully. "Greasy, rotten hospital food. Always tastes like Sasquatch puke to me."

"It was actually not that bad," Samuel replied. "Best meal I've had in a long time, to be honest." That was the truth. In recent years, Samuel had not been taking very good care of himself. His diet consisted mostly of convenience store junk food.

"So, what kind of drugs are they giving you?" Trevor asked. "Anything good?"

"Psych meds. Pills I've never heard of. Standard stuff, according to the nurse."

"Hmm. Probably just antidepressants and lithium, maybe an anticonvulsant...some benzos if you're lucky. Those are nice."

"Benzos?"

"Benzodiazepine," Trevor responded instantly. It was clear to Samuel that Trevor had a vast and comprehensive knowledge of drugs. "Valium, basically. I take a lot for my anxiety. Couldn't function without it."

"Hmm." Samuel was completely uninterested in carrying on a conversation with Trevor. The two men stood in the hallway, facing each other in awkward silence, far past Samuel's threshold. Trevor was content to hover like a stubborn fly, with a silly grin planted on his face. "So," Samuel finally said. "I think I'm going to relax until bed."

"Going back to the room?" Trevor asked. The idea did not appeal to Samuel. He did not want to be trapped in a room with Trevor right now.

"No, gonna watch some TV for a bit." Samuel slipped away.

"Okay, I'll see you later, Sam!" Trevor called after him.

Through the open door, Samuel could see that the television room was once again full. It was clearly the most popular room on the ward. Rather than risking another encounter with Trevor, Samuel decided to take his chances among the media zombies.

Samuel entered the room. A large, outdated television bolted high up on one wall provided the only light. The patients, tightly packed on couches and chairs, basked in its dim glow. The television was still playing music videos. Some patients were staring blankly at the screen, their eyes glazed, their mouths agape. They appeared to be heavily drugged.

On the screen, a nearly naked teenage girl gyrated and twisted in an extremely sexually suggestive dance. The nearly comatose patients drooled, their minds obliterated by the potent chemicals coursing through their veins.

Moving through the room in search of an open seat, Samuel noticed a man on a small couch situated at the back of the room. The man was looking directly at Samuel in an apparent state of awareness that contrasted sharply with the dull mass of people surrounding him. The man smiled, put a hand on the shoulder of the half-awake patient sitting beside him, and gave a shove. The recipient of the not-so-gentle push offered no resistance and simply slid off the couch, ending up in a sitting position on the floor. The eyes of the patient who had been pushed off the couch remained locked on the television the entire time. The smiling man gestured to the now open spot on the couch and beckoned Samuel over.

Samuel, slightly horrified – and slightly amused – sat down beside the man. "Don't worry about the zombies," the man said. "Make yourself at home."

"My name is Brian," the man said. "New here? First time?"

"Yup," Samuel replied. "First time in a pysch ward...and I'm not sure if I really belong here..."

Before Samuel could elaborate on that statement, Brian said, "Yes, you do. You are here for a reason. As soon as I saw you, I knew that. I've been waiting for you, actually."

"Oh?" Samuel said. *Here we go again,* he thought.

"I called for you," Brian said. "And here you are. Welcome!"

Samuel laughed in spite of the seriously bizarre set of circumstances that he had endured on this long, strange day. "You know, after all I've been through, that somehow doesn't surprise me," he said, shaking his head and exhaling.

"You like this shit?" Brian asked, nodding at the television. The gyrating teenager on the screen had been replaced by a comically over-accessorized thug spouting incomprehensible words and gesturing menacingly while posing in front of a sports car.

"Nope. Can't stand it," Samuel replied.

"The zombies *love* it. Look at them eat it up!" With few exceptions, the other patients in the room were still staring blankly at the screen. Samuel felt bad for them.

Samuel made an attempt to change the subject. "How long have you been here?"

"A *long* time. Months. Cops brought me here involuntarily. They're trying to stop me from working. They think that by locking me up they can silence me, prevent the world from hearing my message. Ha! Ridiculous."

Brian turned to face Samuel fully, his eyes wide and radiating intensity. "Now that you are here, the work can truly begin," he said.

"What work?" Samuel asked reluctantly.

"You, my friend, are going to help me write my book...*the* book, *The Final Testament*. We are the chosen ones."

On the television screen, a group of young men sporting black t-shirts and trendy, ridiculous haircuts were pantomiming along to an insipid, tedious rock song. Brian instantly switched gears to comment on the video. "What a goddamn *joke* this music is!" he cried. "Look at these fucking *fools!*"

Brian's previous remarks still echoed in Samuel's head: *Chosen ones...Final Testament...*

"I grew up with *good* music," Brian continued, with a freshly summoned fiery passion. "Zep, Sabbath, Floyd...this new stuff is pure, unmitigated garbage. I'm serious. It makes me literally *sick.*"

A nurse entered the room carrying a tray of pills in tiny cups. She made her way through the room, checking labels and administering medication to each patient in turn. She seemed to know everyone in the room.

She reached the couch where Brian and Samuel were sitting. "Hello, Brian," she said as she handed him his cup. "How are you this evening?"

"I'm good," Brian said, gobbling the pills in one gulp and washing them down with a sip of water poured from a jug the nurse carried. "I'm excellent, actually. One of my disciples arrived. Have you met him yet?" He was, of course, referring to Samuel.

"Who, Sam?" The nurse said. Samuel didn't recall meeting her, yet somehow she knew his name.

"Sam...Samuel...that's a good biblical name," Brian said. "Yes, he's one of my disciples. We were just talking about writing *The Final Testament.*"

"I see," the nurse said, looking at Samuel and gauging his reaction to what Brian had just said. "And how does Sam feel about that?"

Samuel spoke up before Brian could reply. "Sounds like a fun project," he said, giving the nurse a subtle wink.

"Well then, that sounds just fine," the nurse said. "Sam, I have your evening medication."

The nurse handed Samuel his tiny cup. It contained one pill. "This will help you sleep," she said. Samuel swallowed it, washing it down with water the nurse poured into the empty paper cup. "Thank you," he said. The nurse moved on.

"How does it feel to be a disciple of the true messiah?" Brian asked. Samuel found himself playing along. "I suppose it feels...good," he said. "We've got a lot of work to do."

"Damn right, we do!"

A warm sensation was coming over Samuel. The pills were taking effect already. He felt very relaxed, at ease in his own body. All traces of anxiety dissolved. A pleasant, calming blanket of bliss wrapped around him. It was the most comfortable he had been, mentally and physically, in many years. *Wow,* he thought, *this is what contentment feels like.* For someone who had been deeply, clinically depressed for so long, it was like visiting an alien planet.

Samuel and Brian continued their conversation, though most of it was lost to the abyss. Drowsiness was overcoming both of them, and quickly. The medication was powerful. Soon they each retired to their respective rooms and succumbed to deep sleep. Samuel had survived his first day and night in a psychiatric ward.

Three days in, Samuel was fast adapting to life on a psychiatric ward. He began to appreciate the routine, the predictable flow of events, and the elimination of all distractions as he and the doctors focused solely on his mental health. His life had been simplified, his world reduced to a single floor of the hospital. He had even become accustomed to the unusual assortment of characters who populated the ward. They were brethren.

Samuel's body adapted to the chemicals he ingested. The effects were subtle, but the medication seemed to be working. He did, in fact, feel better. His mood had greatly improved, although it was difficult to determine whether it was a result of the pills or simply that the hospital was a safe environment. As a patient, his basic needs were taken care of. He was not required to make many decisions. He was now allowed to wear his own clothes, but his movement in and out of the hospital was still restricted. He was told when to eat and when to sleep.

On a deeper level, the doctors were regulating Samuel's emotions and perceptions through the drugs they prescribed. Unaware, he was becoming institutionalized. Scarier yet, he was losing control of his mind, having surrendered it to a team of psychiatrists and psychologists.

Once a day, Samuel met briefly with Dr. Philips, the psychiatrist he had met upon admittance, to discuss how he was responding to the medication. As his tolerance increased, so did the dosage.

Group therapy sessions helped break up the monotony of the day. These were hosted by a team of psychologists and behavioral specialists, who explored treatment methods beyond the typical psychopharmacological approach. Samuel enjoyed the sessions.

What was conspicuously absent was an examination of the root causes of Samuel's depression. Psychoanalysis – deep penetration and thorough scrutiny of the hidden, inner workings of the mind – was not a real part of Samuel's treatment. There seemed to be an overemphasis – perhaps even complete reliance – on using drugs to treat each and every condition and disorder.

On the third evening of his stay, Samuel had just sat down to eat lunch when something extraordinary and terrifying happened. Seated in front of his assigned tray, across from an elderly man suffering from senile dementia, a new and frightening sensation suddenly washed over him. It was startling in its swift onset and intensity.

Lifting the plastic lid from his tray, Samuel observed roast beef and mashed potatoes...but the appearance of the meal was *off* somehow. The color of the food was too bright, too alive, too *real*. As he gazed at the food, struggling to understand why it suddenly looked so vibrant, so psychedelic, he heard a strange sound, like insects feeding on a fallen corpse in the forest. He looked up and realized instantly that it was the sound of the old man across from him eating, only it was magnified and distorted. It was the soundtrack to a nightmare.

Panic, pure and total, gripped Samuel's mind. *I've been dosed,* he thought. *Poisoned!* What he was experiencing felt just like a bad acid trip. The old man's face was now a warped mask of flesh, throbbing and morphing as Samuel watched. The entire room filled with an inexplicable cloud of dread and menace.

Samuel screamed. The other diners instantly stopped eating and froze. "Help! Help me!" Samuel cried. He was freaking out. A quiet lady with whom Samuel had never spoken before was sitting next to him. "You're having a panic attack," she said calmly.

"I've been poisoned! What are you people giving me?"

The lady seated beside him remained stoic. "Put your head between your legs and breathe, deeply and slowly." It sounded like good advice. Samuel began doing just that.

Finally, a nurse arrived.

"What's wrong, Sam?" the nurse asked.

"He's having a panic attack," the woman beside him said.

"I'm fucking tripping out!" Samuel shrieked, his head still between his legs. He continued taking long, deep breaths.

"Take it easy, Sam," the nurse said. "Everything is fine."

"No, it's *not!*" Sam was hysterical. "The goddamn drugs you're giving me are *poison!* I want out of this fucking place!" A scene such as the one currently playing out in the dining room was far from unusual. It was, after all, a psychiatric ward. The vast majority of the other diners completely ignored Sam's outburst and continued eating.

"Sam, would you like to lie down in your room?" The nurse remained calm as she made the suggestion. Samuel began to cry. "I want to go home," he said, getting out of his seat. The nurse led him out of the dining room.

In the hall, Samuel's episode continued. He looked at the nurse and saw a mad scientist, or perhaps a deranged butcher, leading him to a dark dungeon somewhere in the bowels of the hospital, full of torture implements and certain, excruciating, doom. "What are you going to do to me?" he begged.

The nurse's expression never changed, but to Samuel's eyes, in the condition he was in, things were moving beneath her skin – bugs, alien parasites, *creatures* – causing her face to bubble and stretch in obscene ways. Samuel moaned. "Water," he gasped. "I need water. I think I'm dying."

"You aren't dying," the nurse reassured him. "You might be having a reaction to the medication, but it will pass. You'll be just fine." Her words were the antidote. Just like that, Samuel began to feel better. He still felt like he was on a psychedelic trip of some sort – colors were still too vivid, and the walls seemed to breathe, but the panic had dissipated.

The nurse brought Samuel to his room. He sat on the bed and she brought him a cup of water. He drank it and felt better still. "Whew," he sighed, "I think this medication is too strong for me. I really thought I was going to pass out, or freak out...or maybe die. I couldn't breathe! I don't think I've ever been so scared in my life."

"That sounds exactly like a panic attack," the nurse said. It was the first time Samuel had ever experienced one. "I guess I was in the right place, then!" he said, the irony not completely lost to him.

From behind the extended curtain between beds, movement and a shrill voice arose. "Yup, sounds like a panic attack!" Trevor pulled back the curtain and inserted himself into the moment. "I should know," he continued. "I've been having them my whole life. A real pain in the ass!"

Samuel groaned internally. *I'm too high for this*, he thought.

"Hello, Trevor," the nurse said. "How are you today?"

"Today has been better," Trevor replied. He held his bandaged wrists out for the nurse and Samuel to see. "Not as much pain in my arms, but I'm still having negative thoughts. I don't think I'm ready to be discharged quite yet."

"That's something you need to discuss with your doctor," the nurse said.

"Will I be seeing her today?" Trevor said. "I think my lorazepam needs to be increased..."

"I don't know, Trevor," the nurse said, exasperated. "Right now, I'm tending to Samuel. He isn't feeling well."

"I'm okay...I think," Samuel said.

"He'll be fine," Trevor said. "It was just a panic attack. I almost *died!*"

"Yes, I know," the nurse said.

"Really, I think I'll be fine," Samuel insisted. His sense perceptions were quickly returning to normal. The iridescent tracers and disorienting visual vibrations had disappeared. The sound reaching his ears no longer carried an unsettling, demonic resonance. He still felt lightheaded – a little giddy and short of breath – but he no longer felt in imminent danger of losing his mind. For a few moments there, Samuel *did* feel his grip on reality, and his very identity, slipping away.

"I'd really like to step outside and get some fresh air," Samuel said.

"Are you sure you're allowed to do that?" Trevor said.

"I'm not a prisoner," Samuel snapped.

"I'll have to check your file," the nurse said. "Before you can leave the ward you need clearance from your doctor."

"He could be a danger to himself...or others," Trevor said, a touch of glee in his voice.

"I'm not going to hurt myself – or anyone else. I just need air...and sun...and a few minutes to gather myself. The walls of this place are starting to close in on me."

"Trips off ward need to be cleared with your doctor," the nurse reiterated. "Leaving the hospital against doctor's advice could jeopardize your treatment."

"I've heard that before," Samuel said. "Forget it. I'll take a nap or something."

"That's an excellent idea. If you need anything, let me know." The nurse left the room.

Trevor was sitting on his bed staring at Samuel. Despite the lack of eyebrows, Trevor still managed to convey a look of serious concern. "What happened to you?" he asked.

"I think I had a bad reaction to the medication,"

Samuel said, lying down on his bed. "Scary stuff. Felt like I was on LSD or something."

"That happened to me when I first started taking antidepressants." It was virtually impossible for Trevor to avoid talking about himself at every opportunity. "Zoloft, I think. Or was it Effexor? Maybe Celexa or Prozac. Actually, now that I think about it, I think it was Cymbalta..."

It was too tedious for Samuel. He had to escape. "You know, I doubt I'll be able to sleep," he said, rising from the bed. "Gonna find a book to read." He was out the door and halfway down the hall before Trevor had a chance to respond. He went directly to the lounge.

The staff called the recreation lounge the 'quiet room.' On this day, however, Samuel could hear someone playing the piano as he approached. The music was loud and wild. It sounded like someone was bashing the keys randomly and singing – screeching – at the tops of their lungs in accompaniment. Samuel hesitated at the door before deciding to enter.

Brian was seated at the piano. He was flailing and bobbing, his eyes closed, as he hammered passionately – relentlessly, on the keys. The music was awful, the lyrics asinine. He was, apparently, making it up as he went along. *"Gonna lead 'em to the promised land, gonna hold 'em in a mighty hand..."* Brian sang on, unaware that someone had entered the room.

"Sounds good," Samuel lied as he took a seat in an easy chair by the window. Brian opened his eyes. "Thanks, man," he said, still poking at keys arbitrarily. "I'm working on an album. It'll be released at the same time as *The Final Testament.* The faithful will be able to listen to the songs while they read the truth – a full, sensory experience!"

Brian finally, mercifully, stopped playing and turned

on the piano stool to face Samuel. "How have you been, brother?" he asked, his voice soaked in earnest concern. Samuel had to seriously ponder the question before he could answer. He had not fully recovered from his drug-induced delirium. The world still retained a surreal veneer. "It's been a weird day," he said at last.

Brian smiled knowingly and nodded. "Three days in, right?"

"Yes."

"I bet you've been experiencing some unusual...sensations. Freaky, psychedelic stuff. True?"

"That is true," Samuel said with a hint of trepidation.

"You probably think the feelings are a side effect of the medication they're giving you...at least, that's what the doctors and nurses are going to say." Brian leaned in, his face stern, his eyes steely. "Don't believe them," he whispered.

"Uh, okay...but I *did* have a reaction to the pills, I think..."

Brian laughed heartily. "No, my brother, it wasn't the pills," he said. "You've been reborn. Three days ago the old you perished and then you were resurrected. Welcome to Christ consciousness. You now inhabit an astral body as well as a vessel of flesh and bone."

Samuel opened his mouth in an attempt to reply...but no words came. He simply stared at Brian, baffled, a quizzical expression stamped on his face.

"How does it feel?" Brian asked. "Is this your first miracle?"

Gazing out the window at the world beyond the hospital walls, Samuel sighed. He had a sudden urge to jump right through the glass. He visualized himself hitting the street running, not stopping until he was far, far away from the psych ward – far from hyper-religious and perhaps dangerously delusional Brian, far from the unsettling sickness percolating within Trevor's shaven head, far from the nurses and doctors and pills. The madness was viral. The depression that had originally brought him in seemed tame in comparison.

Brian was still preaching, still delivering his impassioned, lunatic sermon: "*The Final Testament* will be the last book ever written. It is the final chapter of human history, in this world and the next. You and I will finally reveal the hidden truth of this existence – of *all* existence, spanning this dimension and a vast multitude of others. Aren't you *excited?* The time for the ultimate revelation is upon us...and you and I are messengers! We've been chosen."

"Amazing," Samuel said, still fantasizing about his grand escape. He settled for a minor evasion. "Listen, Brian, I'm still not feeling well. I think I'll try to get some sleep."

"I understand. Resurrection is a painful, tiring process. Go rest. Tomorrow we'll start writing..."

"Okay, see ya." Samuel was on his way out of the room before Brian could finish.

"Bless you, brother." Brian made some obscure gesture of anointment that Samuel neither recognized nor understood.

In the hall, Samuel's sense of confinement increased. An anxious restlessness grew within him. To his horror, he could feel another panic attack approaching. Its arrival was preceded by an awful tingling at the back of his head – an unpleasant throb deep within his brain – and a cold shudder like the embrace of an invisible, icy spectre. Before the wave of panic overwhelmed and immobilized him, Samuel rushed down the hall toward the nurses' desk.

"It's happening again," he said to the first nurse he encountered, his breath short, his brow sweating.

"What is, Sam?" the nurse asked.

"The drugs..." Samuel stammered. "I'm freaking out again. Whatever it is you guys are giving me here, it's too strong. I'm having a bad reaction."

"Would you like some water? Have you tried lying down?"

"I want to see a doctor. I want to feel like myself again."

"Your doctor is currently unavailable."

"I'm losing my mind!" Samuel shouted. "Don't you understand what I'm telling you? *I want to see a fucking doctor!*" The outburst caught the attention of every nurse and patient within earshot. All sound and motion on the ward suddenly ceased. All eyes were upon Samuel.

"Sam, you need to relax," the nurse said, rising slowly. "I can't do anything for you if you're agitated." Tears were beginning to well in Samuel's eyes. "Please, help me," he whimpered.

"I can give you something to calm you down," the nurse said. "I see here the doctor has prescribed Ativan for you, to be taken as needed..."

"No more drugs!" Samuel protested. His body was vibrating, as if electrified by an unseen power source. His brain was buzzing with psychedelic impressions. The last thing he wanted was to ingest more chemicals.

"Then I suggest you lie down and do some breathing exercises," the nurse stated bluntly.

What am I doing here? Samuel thought. He walked away from the nurses' desk without another word. At the door to his room he looked in and saw Trevor in his usual spot on the far bed, reading a magazine and absentmindedly running a hand over his bald head.

Samuel made an instant decision. Instead of entering the hospital room, he kept walking down the hall, all the way to the big doors which separated the psychiatric ward from the rest of the hospital. A nurse saw him as he reached out to push the doors open. "Where are you going, Sam?" she asked. "Are you allowed to leave the ward?"

Samuel stopped to face her. "Yes," he simply said.

Samuel walked right out of the hospital and into the open air of a cool evening. He had not been outside in three days. The fresh air was invigorating. The hallucinatory fog in Samuel's head began to lift. He moved his legs. He moved his arms. His body responded to the commands his brain issued. He was *alive*...and knew it.

Falling into a comfortable stride, Samuel tuned into his surroundings. He felt an intimate connection to the world around him – a renewed appreciation for nature, for the city he lived in and its inhabitants, for his body and mind...for life itself. Something gentle and glorious stirred within him. Samuel looked up at the night sky. It appeared to him, in this moment of awakening, to be wide open to the space beyond, as if the atmosphere had bled away, leaving the cosmos bare and exposed. The stars were so bright and close that they seemed to be hovering mere feet above him. His thoughts rose from his head and expanded until they filled the universe...and the universe filled him.

Samuel kept walking until he reached his apartment building. It may have taken hours or a single instant, he could not be sure. He entered the building and went to his apartment. It was as he had left it, yet it seemed so unfamiliar. His furniture and possessions were exactly where they should have been. He could even see the remains of the last meal that he had prepared before leaving for the hospital sitting undisturbed on the table. The blank canvas still hung on the wall. The gun still sat under the papers on the end table.

It was he himself, Samuel realized, who had changed.

Where once he felt only despair and emptiness, he now felt hope and purpose. Drive and determination replaced apathetic lethargy. Confidence replaced insecurity. He had been to the edge – the very brink of destruction, and had fought his way back to the light, along the way discovering a previously unknown resiliency and strength that existed within his character. *Perhaps*, he thought, *I've been resurrected after all.*

Inspired like never before, Samuel approached the blank canvas hanging on the wall. He was no longer intimidated by its empty, white surface. Instead, he saw it for what it truly was – a wide open expanse of infinite creative possibilities. He picked up a brush, opened a tube of acrylic color, and began to paint.

The Product

"This product has the power to transform lives! We must never forget that what we sell is no mere beverage. This product is a *real* energy drink. It is the Holy Spirit distilled – miracle in a can!"

The speaker addressed the conference attendees with passion and conviction, like a charismatic preacher before his congregation. The assembled crowd of employees, acolytes and adoring minions sat in rapt silence, completely enthralled and hanging on every word. They had gathered at this conference to hear the CEO deliver his vision of the company's future. There had been rumors and intimations of a radical new direction.

The CEO continued his speech. He was really on fire now:

"We are on the threshold of a new era," he said with calculated confidence and sincerity. "We in this beautiful family of investors, merchants, and consumers are well aware of the glorious power of this product. In one way or another, it has transformed the lives of everyone in this room. The time has come for us – with God's help, of course – to take what we have experienced and share it with the world. The time has come to go *global!*" This inspired a raucous burst of applause from the audience. They were intoxicated on the speaker's words, gobbling them up like candied opiates.

"Many of you have been with us from the very beginning. You are familiar with the story of how I was chosen to lead this company. You have heard me speak often of the divine revelation I received and how, using my formidable entrepreneurial spirit, I embarked on my mission to bring a faith-infused energy drink to the market. It has been a challenging journey, but with God's help, our product is now available nationwide...but it is to you, my foot-soldiers, my real *warriors,* that I owe the most gratitude."

"You are not simply salespeople, you are true disciples. Through you, the product reaches more and more consumers. The network expands, lives are transformed, and, let's be frank, we make *money!*" The last statement drew a delirious roar of approval from the crowd.

"There's nothing wrong with making money," the CEO said earnestly. "Never let anyone convince you otherwise. Making money is a very good thing. It's good for us, our families, the economy...it's *all* good! Don't be ashamed of making money – it is a sign of God's grace and presence in your life."

"We must never forget that our product is a wonderful innovation in beverage technology. We are providing people with the world's first totally organic, faith-based energy drink. We are evangelists who have been charged with the duty of transforming lives."

The CEO lowered his voice, now speaking in a hushed, serious tone. "I think the world is ready for us, I truly do. I think our time has come. Some of you have been speculating about what I am about to reveal. The truth is that yes, our team of designers and beverage engineers have been working around the clock – to the brink of total exhaustion – on our new line of drinks. I am here today to announce the newest addition to our arsenal, the product that we will take to the masses on a global scale."

The CEO paused, gazing out upon the captivated audience, then, with great, dramatic effect, pointed to a large projection screen suspended on the wall behind him.

"Introducing..." Triumphant music erupted from the auditorium speakers. The image of an over-sized black and red aluminum can appeared on the screen, filling it almost entirely. *"Revelation!"*

A collective gasp of astonishment rose from the audience. The effect of the unveiling was grand, the excitement of the crowd palpable, as if powerful currents of electricity pulsed among them.

One of the conference attendees was particularly affected – a young, enthusiastic, true-believer salesman from some small, mid-western town. His name was Darryl, and he had traveled hundreds of miles to be at this event. He was a relatively new addition to the team – a recent convert, as it were – having joined the company only a few months previously.

Darryl was extremely loyal and fully dedicated to the company and its products. "This beverage changed my life!" he was fond of telling anyone who would listen. "I am living proof that miracles are real!"

Before discovering the company's brand of energy drinks, Darryl had led an unfulfilled life: single, under educated, uninspired, unmotivated, and toiling away as a part time clerk at a convenience store. In his spare time, he played video games and watched DVDs at home in his tiny bachelor apartment. The occasional night out for drinks with his few friends was the highlight of his limited social life. He had not been unhappy, simply stagnant, uninspired, and directionless.

The crucial turning point arrived unpredictably one typical evening at work. It was a slow night at the convenience store, the kind of night where the very nature of time seems to distort, stretching out each hour to an eternity. Darryl sat behind the counter, mindlessly flipping through a magazine and casting desperate glances at the clock.

Darryl was in agony, anxious for his shift to end. Time slowly passed like thick mud through a straw. Darryl felt the weight of infinite eons crushing his spirit. He began to feel very sleepy. "Ugh," he groaned as he stood up to stretch. He wandered over to the cooler in search of something to drink. He spotted a beverage he had seen before but had never tried. It was a popular energy drink in a large, gaudily colored can. The label promised "5 hours of vigor!"

"I could sure use that," Darryl muttered as he popped the tab. He raised the can to his lips and guzzled the sparkling fluid. Instantly, a warm, pleasurable sensation surged in his chest. He could actually feel a strange energy enter his body, igniting each nerve as it spread to his limbs, culminating in an explosion of tingling vibrations and exquisite electricity in his head. He was invigorated. He felt powerful, confident, clear-headed, and simply wonderful.

"Wow!" Darryl exclaimed. "That is good stuff!"

As the days and weeks passed, he consumed more and more of the energy drink until it was a constant presence in his life. The more he drank, the better he felt about himself and his place in the world. "You have *got* to try this stuff," he told his friends. "It's great. Changed my life, actually. I've never felt so strong...and *clear*! I've got energy and clarity like never before. Wish I had known about it sooner!"

It wasn't long before he decided that he should graduate from consumer to vendor of the product he loved. The beverage was manufactured and distributed by a rather small but fast-growing company led by an enigmatic CEO who combined shrewd business tactics with a pseudo-religious approach. The CEO was adored by his employees, who were organized in a classic pyramid scheme model. Like Darryl, they all consumed the beverage.

Soon, Darryl had his start-up kit and was on the team, pitching the product – and the opportunity to join the company – to friends, family, local stores, and anyone who gave him a chance to speak. He made friends in the company, and eventually even a little money. He felt a sense of purpose and belonging for the first time in his life. He even made the long drive to attend the annual conference, which is where we find him now, deliriously electrified by the unveiling of the new product.

The whole crowd was thrilled. They spoke in animated reverence:

"It's amazing! I *love* the name and the design of the can!"

"This is gonna be a real hit. I can't wait to start selling Revelation to the folks back home!"

"I'm so lucky to be part of this wonderful company. Thank God for the product!"

Many of the attendees were openly weeping with joy. The CEO spoke again:

"Oh yes, Revelation Energy is the real deal. Friends, we are on the cusp of an incredible victory. I predict that this product will rocket our beloved company into the stratosphere. This is the product that will help us not only compete with the major beverages, but some day dominate the market. Are you ready for that? Are you ready for the big leagues? Are you ready to go *global*?"

A roar of unanimous approval. The audience was near frenzy.

"Now, as you know, we are still a family...a family that values hard work and dedication. Each year, we recognize the contributions of a select few who exemplify these values. There is, among you who are gathered here today, one such individual – an employee of outstanding merit and integrity – who truly deserves recognition. I'd like to honor this person today, right now, in front of all of you."

Another of the CEO's trademark dramatic pauses. The anticipation in the audience grew. The CEO's intense gaze passed over the crowd. Finally, he spoke:

"Darryl Sanders, stand up, please. Stand up and be recognized by your peers." Darryl sat shocked, disbelieving. *Me?* he silently mouthed. "Yes, you, Darryl," said the CEO. "Stand up and be acknowledged!"

Darryl was dumbfounded. The lady sitting beside him placed a hand on his shoulder and smiled. "Go ahead, honey," she said, urging him to stand and bask in the applause. "You deserve it." Darryl stood, and the applause grew to a crescendo, swallowing him up in its undeniable, irresistible force. Darryl grinned widely and waved, utterly ecstatic as he bathed in his moment of glory. *This is the best day of my life*, he thought.

"Congratulations, Darryl, and thank you for everything you have done for this company," said the CEO from the stage. "We have prepared a special plaque for you. At the conclusion of this presentation, come see me. I'd like to personally present it to you."

The rest of the conference passed in a blur for Darryl. He felt like he was in a movie or a dream. When the presentations and speeches concluded, the attendees gathered in a large dining area for a celebratory meal. Darryl meekly approached the CEO, who was still loitering near the stage speaking to his assistants.

The CEO noticed Darryl as he neared and held out his hand, smiling warmly. "Darryl, it's a real pleasure to meet you."

"Thank you, sir! It's an honor to meet *you*," Darryl gushed as they shook hands firmly. "This company means everything to me and I admire you so much. Thank you, sir. Thank you."

Up close, the CEO looked even sharper than he had appeared on stage – square-jawed, slick-haired, with unnaturally white teeth, bright eyes, and a huge, confident grin. His expensive suit was crisp and spotless. He wore gold and diamond-encrusted jewelry around his neck and on his fingers. The CEO looked almost *too* perfect, like a model or a movie star.

"Darryl, I'd like to talk to you in private. Care to join me for a drink in my room? There's much I'd like to discuss with you."

"Of course! I'd love to!"

The CEO led Darryl away with a strong, assured hand on his shoulder. They left the conference room and walked the halls of the hotel.

"It is young men like you, Darryl, who make this company what it is. Without pure, uncorrupted souls like yours, we couldn't succeed in the highly competitive beverage market. In fact, we couldn't even manufacture this wonderful product that we, as a family, have grown to love and depend upon."

Darryl thought that was a strange thing to say – *pure, uncorrupted souls* – but he remained quiet and respectful as the CEO continued, "You were chosen to be honored today, and you have also been chosen to contribute to the future of this company in a very real, tangible way. How does that make you feel?"

"Honored. I feel honored...and happy."

"Excellent, Darryl. I'm glad to hear that. Here's my room. Let's discuss this further, shall we?"

The CEO stopped in front of his room and used a card key to open the door. He encouraged Darryl to enter and then followed him in. The heavy door shut behind them. Darryl was confused by what he saw. It was if he had suddenly stepped onto the set of a low-budget horror movie. The room was lit entirely by candles, seemingly hundreds of them, placed on every surface and in clusters on the floor.

Hooded figures in black and red robes stood motionless, lurking in the shadowy corners of the room. Darryl realized they were chanting in unison. It was the most eerie, otherworldly sound he had ever heard. On the floor, a large pentagram had been painted in blood-red, surrounded by weird symbols and glyphs.

Darryl became frightened – seriously, enormously, mortally frightened. "Sometimes, Darryl," said the CEO as he drew a dagger from a hidden sheath, "one needs to make sacrifices in order for the company to succeed."

The Observatory

The ocean is a writhing, frothing, convulsing beast. The night sky is an oppressive, impenetrable, black canopy, filled with the lunatic shimmering of a legion of stars. On the western Canadian shore, the air is sharp and cool. In my imagination, I move across the beach as if I had just been born, spawned from the water like some scaled, segmented, creeping probe.

A short crawl through the sand, sheer rock walls dominate the landscape. Upon these rocks, perched high above the vast and lonesome beach, sits a massive domed structure – the observatory. I penetrate the structure and peer inside. I see a massive telescope aimed through a slit in the dome at the unfathomable abyss beyond. There is a man with a ravenous mind gazing through the eyepiece on the small end. The man's name is Gordon. He is an astronomer. This is his story.

Gordon had been a bright child – shy, socially awkward, slightly strange, but *smart*. How that served him, I wish I knew. He was the only child of loving and devoted parents. Early on, he had developed a love of learning and a fascination with nature and the cosmos. His parents had supported his interests and encouraged him to pursue a life in academics. He had succeeded in school and became what he thought he was – a serious, solitary, dedicated man of science.

At the age of 33, we find Gordon here, alone in the cavernous depths of the Moonsword Observatory. I can see him now, pacing the upper deck of the facility, tossing an occasional, tentative glance toward the telescope. He is clearly afraid of something. I can see it in the way his eyes twitch in their sockets, like eggs about to hatch. I imagine bizarre mutations being born from those eyes. I imagine terrors beyond space and time emerging from that mind.

Gordon is deeply troubled. Last night, while studying unusual deep space objects, a true anomaly appeared. In the constellation of Virgo, a ghostly white worm had wiggled into view under Gordon's watch. It was a beautiful sight. The worm's body emitted tendrils of pure light as it pulsated and moved through space.

The creature rolled and squirmed in rhythmic motion, as if performing an intricate dance, before suddenly dissipating in a burst of soft, glowing fibers. It was sublime, magnificent...and totally irrational. All that Gordon had been taught about the universe told him that what he had witnessed should not exist. His education – his expertise and knowledge – conflicted with what he had just experienced directly through his senses.

Gordon went home that night feeling exhilarated, yet slightly ill. Had he really seen a ghost worm somewhere out there in the depths of space? Had he perhaps imagined it? It occurred to him that he had probably been spending too many solitary days and nights in the observatory. Too much time entirely isolated and focused purely on work is bound to have some negative consequences on one's mental health. Gordon carefully considered this possibility and chose to accept it as the most likely cause of the unlikely incident. As he lay in bed, he felt something resembling relief as his thoughts dissolved and his consciousness ebbed away. He drifted numbly into a dreamless sleep.

Upon waking, Gordon's first thought was of the strange sight he had beheld the night before: the white worm dancing in space. Gordon's mind was filled with the image. With his eyes still closed he could see its ethereal form maneuvering in the void between galaxies, majestic, *unreal.*

Gordon opened his eyes and, for a moment, the white worm was still visible, superimposed upon the reality of his bedroom wall. He reached out instinctively, his fingers hungry to touch the unknown. The white worm faded away. Gordon got out of bed. He proceeded with his morning routine.

Let's join Gordon now in the observatory, at the exact moment when we first encountered him, pacing the facility, tossing tentative glaces at the telescope. He is afraid, you see, because he has once again seen something entirely implausible while using the sophisticated scientific instrument. He had been willing to accept one such anomaly - the ghostly white worm - as an artifact of an overworked, overtired mind, but to have another inexplicable experience after a good night's rest was more than a little disturbing.

I will try to describe what Gordon saw, though it may be difficult. It happened while he was studying the same area in the constellation of Virgo as the previous night. He saw what was to be expected in that region: the stars, galaxies, and other celestial bodies that others had charted before.

These objects, though fascinating and beautiful in their own right, were not what truly interested him. His greatest desire – the ultimate fulfillment of his life's work – was to find something *new*, something never before seen, something extraordinary that would change our perception of the cosmos...something that would make him famous in the scientific community.

It is important to understand that when Gordon is in the observatory using the equipment, his voracious mind sprouts tentacles of thought and the telescope becomes an extension of his consciousness. The observatory is fully computerized. The images it gathers are displayed and easily viewed on high-definition monitors, but Gordon prefers to observe through the eyepiece. It's more personal.

Through the telescope's lenses, Gordon extends his awareness like the probe at the beginning of this story. He wanders the cosmos, pierces the veil, and lingers like a stranger in the infinite halls of the great chambers of space. In this state, his mind and environment are united. As within, so beyond. In this state, he encountered a second anomaly.

Watching, waiting, carefully observing...Gordon's body was forgotten, irrelevant. His entire being was focused on that distant point in space, trembling in anticipation like one giant nerve.

Then he saw it! A horizontal slit appeared in the midst of nothingness, a widening tear in the fabric of spacetime. It opened, slowly, deliberately. A dark spot became visible in its center, surrounded by a swirling circle of unusual colors. These features rested on a sea of pink-streaked white.

Gordon quickly realized then that he was looking at an enormous eye. The width of that anomalous ocular opening must have spanned light years of interstellar space. Can you imagine Gordon's shock? As his mind struggled to process the sight, he remained at the telescope, his eye on the eyepiece looking into the giant eye in the heavens. It was fractal...and comical.

Gordon blinked. The big eye blinked. Gordon allowed himself to laugh. He pulled away from the instrument. His internal dialogue became externalized:

"Well, Gordon, you may very well be losing your mind." It made him feel better to talk to himself in such a way. He attempted to maintain a semblance of control, but feared that his mind was in imminent danger of fracturing completely.

"Just take it easy and get a hold of yourself. There *must* be a rational explanation." Gears spun in his head.

Wheels turned, but found no traction. His mind struggled to reconcile what he had seen with what he believed to be reality.

"I am a man of *science*. Educated. Erudite. Sober. Sane." The words resonated pleasantly in Gordon's ears. He was soothing himself effectively. He ran sweaty fingers through greasy hair.

"Confirmation – that's what I need. I'll get the boys in Australia to check it out." It was a good idea. It would be easy to make a call to his peers and have them train their instruments on the same spot to validate his sighting.

Gordon paused. He paced the cramped room, scratching his stubbly, red face with twitchy nervous hands.

"No, no, no...can't do that. What if I'm wrong? What if they don't find anything there?" He picked at his left eyebrow, plucking hairs and examining them. "I'd be humiliated, discredited. My reputation would be ruined."

Gordon could feel the cramped interior of the observatory closing in on him. The instruments and gauges choked the air out of his lungs. Suddenly, claustrophobia descended on him like a bird of prey. He stopped pacing and stood still, his mind reeling.

"You're overthinking again, Gordon. Relax. You are a man of science. Gather more data." He slowly approached the telescope, which now looked phallic and obscene. He lowered his eye to the eyepiece. Contact. The universe again filled his head with its wondrous, horrifying sights.

The telescope was still fixed on the same spot. The eye was no longer there. Only the familiar, expected objects were present. The black void of deep space occupied the region where the eye's immense, ominous, aperture had opened mere moments ago and peered into Gordon's soul. Sweet relief...it was followed closely by a strange, subtle disappointment. "Whew," Gordon said, still looking through the eyepiece, "thought maybe I was coming unglued."

As Gordon was about to pull away, movement caught his attention – again, there was activity in the region where he had seen the eye. Gordon gasped. Great clouds of cosmic dust were forming in real time as he watched. Purple and pink nebulous structures billowed and expanded, creating complex designs.

"No!" Gordon cried. "That can't be!" The clouds of cosmic dust began to form words, as if guided by the hand of an omniscient creator: *Hi Gordon!*

Gordon promptly pulled away from the eyepiece. "Oh no...oh no!" he shrieked in distress. He sat in a chair and put his head in trembling hands. He began to sob quietly.

"It's over. I'm finished." Gordon sensed movement behind him – someone else was in the room. Gordon raised his head, looked around, and saw a man standing there. The man was smiling. The man was me.

"Hi, Gordon," I said. "Don't be sad. Everything's fine." I reached over and put my hand on Gordon's shoulder. I felt bad for him and didn't like seeing him in such a state. I liked him.

"Who are you?" Gordon asked.

"The writer of this story," I told him. No need to lie. He could handle the truth.

"I don't understand...how can that be? What does it mean?!"

"That's a good question, and I'm not sure I have a satisfactory answer. It has something to do with the observatory, though. I'm sure of that."

"Am I one of your characters?"

"Yes, you are, but so am I. We are both characters...and we are both observers." It was hard to explain. I didn't want to scare him any more than he already was. The bizarre situation was even starting to scare *me* a little. Is it getting too weird around here? Let's try to resolve this.

"The telescope," I said to Gordon, "it allows you to peer out into the universe, to explore its hidden secrets. It's an amazing tool. What if, while looking out, something is also looking in at you?" Gordon was beginning to understand. I, too, was beginning to understand.

"So, it's like I'm somehow the observer *and* the observed." Gordon rubbed his chin philosophically. "Wow. Heavy."

"Heavy indeed," I said. "In this story *I* have become the subject as well as the observer. It's a closed system, a holographic, fractal miniverse." We sat pondering in silence for a few moments. I began to wonder if the words I had chosen were adequate.

"I didn't mean to upset you," I continued. "For that, I am sorry. I simply wanted to tell a story."

"It's okay. It's been fun. I was worried that it might get *really* freaky, but it wasn't so bad." Gordon smiled for the first time. It was nice to see. "What now?" he asked. "Will we see each other again?"

"I think so. I really do. For now, though, I think we should both move on. You have a lot of work to do, I suspect. A lot of discoveries to make, as do I." It was a little sad saying goodbye. Gordon had become a friend. I reached out my hand and he took it. We shook firmly and with warmth.

"Alright then," Gordon said. "I'll see you later."

"Bye, Gordon," I smiled.

I contemplated various ways to finish the story before choosing an old, reliable standard:

The End

The Calling

The man awoke in the desert with no recollection of his past or identity. A scorching wind swept across the desolate plains. Clouds of dust billowed and undulated as if animated by spectral entities. The man was lying prone on the hard, dusty ground. Consciousness returned to his body in a slow insertion. Overhead, the sun raged and throbbed, bathing him in its intense, unforgiving heat, indifferent to his predicament.

The man sat up. A sharp pain instantly alerted him to a problem in his lower back. He cried aloud as a bolt of agony shot up to his reeling brain. He reached back and explored his lower spine with trembling fingers. He was shocked to discover a small, metallic lump under the skin attached to a vertebra a few inches above his butt. He immediately understood at least one aspect of his frightening and inexplicable situation – *I've been implanted*, he realized. He found a mental compartment in which to store this disturbing bit of information.

The dense fog that clouded the man's mind began to clear. He could still not access his memories, but his clarity of sensory perception was growing, his awareness of the environment increasing. He looked around and discovered that he was sitting on a patch of earth in a scrappy, remote area. Bizarre, beautiful, and dangerous desert flora sparsely dotted the landscape. The intermittent islands of stubborn life were juxtaposed strongly with the vast expanses of dry, dead ground. It was unfamiliar and alien territory.

Thirst, strong and desperate, clawed at the man's throat. *I need water*, he thought. The fearful nature of his body's demand was sufficient impetus. He gathered his strength and attempted to stand up, making it to a crouching position before a wave of vertigo caused him to nearly pass out. He paused, his hands on his knees and his head down, while his brain wavered on the edge of deep black nothingness. The man could feel his consciousness flickering like a loose light bulb.

Finally, the man was able to get to his feet. Something in his peripheral vision glinted in the harsh light of the sun and caught his eye – a small object resting at the base of a strange, spiky, tentacled plant which sprouted from the desert floor like a ragged talon. The man approached the plant and bent down to examine the object. It was a small box roughly the size of his fist with a lid secured by a metal clasp.

The man picked up the box, hesitated for a moment, then released the clasp and opened it. Inside sat a tiny, transparent bottle and a piece of paper. The man picked up the bottle. It was full of little white pills. The label on the bottle read: *Hydration Tablets*. The man examined the paper. On it was a typed note, which read: *Take one of these once a day if you want to survive.*

"Well, isn't that interesting," the man said. He looked around again, scanning the brutal, inhospitable environment. For as far as he could see stretched nothing but desert, shimmering in the heat. The man's thirst was growing. He pondered the risk of taking one of the pills. *Whoever left me here could have killed me already,* he thought. *If they wanted me dead, I would be.* The logic seemed sound enough. He opened the bottle and popped a pill into his mouth.

The pill instantly dissolved upon his tongue. Within moments, the man began to feel better. He was no longer dizzy and no longer shaky, but he was still hot and hungry. The sun was almost directly overhead, indicating to him that it was midday. It would be a while before the coming evening brought relief from the cruel and relentless radiance of the sun. "I need shade...and food," the man said to himself. The complete absence of any signs of human beings or their habitations made the man feel a little wild in the head. It was spooky. Talking to himself made him feel better. "I better get moving," he said.

The man then became aware of his clothing. He was wearing a simple white T-shirt and a pair of loose-fitting cargo shorts. On his feet were a good pair of rugged hiking shoes. He was relieved to find that he was dressed appropriately for the climate and conditions. He put the small box in one of the spacious pockets of his shorts.

In the distance loomed a large mountain range, its appearance hazy and ethereal as it shimmered on the horizon. "I'd be safer there," the man said. "More shade, more shelter, more food." He set his sights on the mountains and focused his attention on reaching them. His immediate problems of health and safety had temporarily displaced the troubling issues of who and where he was, survival trumping his newfound identity crisis.

The man walked. The desert received him in its harsh embrace. For nearly an hour the man encountered nothing but cacti, rocks, and the occasional skittering lizard. The small reptiles zipped in and out of view before the man's brain could fully register their presence. A large bird of prey appeared far overhead. It swooped and circled as it followed the man's progress through the brutal landscape. "I'm not dead yet," the man said. "Go find something else to hunt." The bird screeched, as if in response.

Just ahead, the man spotted something anomalous. It appeared to be a wooden box affixed to a pole. "What do we have here?" the man said. It looked like a mailbox in the middle of nowhere. He moved in to get a better look, but before he could get any closer, an eerie sound rose sharply and caused him to freeze in his tracks. It sounded like an electrical transformer and emanated from everywhere and nowhere at once, its volume increasing until the man's head began to ache.

As the man watched, the air around the mailbox began to ripple and waver. It was like the heat effect of the desert, only much, much more intense and localized in the immediate vicinity of the box. The rippling, like the sound, grew in intensity and, for a moment, the desert and the distant mountains were replaced with an urban street setting...or more accurately, the two scenes were superimposed.

Suddenly, there was a vehicle beside the mailbox. It appeared instantly, as if it had been cloaked the moment before – or as if it had been teleported from some distant location. The vehicle was long, black, and apparently armored, like a cross between a stretch limousine and a tank. A door on its side opened and a man in a dark suit stepped out. "Hello, Philip," the man in the suit said.

Philip, the amnesiac thought. *My name is Philip.*

The man in the suit opened the mailbox and put something slender inside. "You'll need this," he said to Philip. The man in the suit shut the mailbox and entered the vehicle. The vehicle instantly disappeared in a flash of light. Philip stood for a moment, dumbfounded, before he approached the mailbox.

Inside the mailbox, Philip discovered the suited man's offering – a large envelope. He opened it and found a single sheet of paper. It was a map.

The map was a topographical representation of the desert and the nearby mountain range. This was made clear to Philip by a star near the center with the words 'You are here' written above it. "That's helpful," Philip said, "but where the heck is *here*?"

Philip studied the map carefully. There was another star near the top of the map, marking a location somewhere in the mountains. Philip was no cartographer, but to his untrained eyes, the terrain between his location and the other starred location appeared to be relatively flat, at least up to the tightly spaced curved lines of the mountain range which indicated a steep ascent. "Is that where I'm supposed to go?" Philip asked himself...and the now-dematerialized man in the vehicle that had popped in and out of view like a vessel between dimensions. "I suppose I'll play along. Somehow I get the feeling I don't have a choice."

The sun had descended in the sky considerably. The day was slipping away quickly, late afternoon transitioning rapidly into early evening. Philip examined the map again in an attempt to comprehend its scale. Near the bottom of the map, Philip noticed what appeared to be a deep wash – he remembered crossing the wash not long after he had set out on his hike through the desert after awakening. Using his fingers, he crudely measured the distance between it and the star indicating his current location. He then measured the apparent distance from his own star to the star in the mountain range. "No way I'll get there before dark," he correctly surmised. "I need to find somewhere to spend the night." Philip folded the map neatly and put it in a deep pocket of his shorts. He walked on toward the mountains, leaving behind the strange mailbox.

Philip hiked through the desert until bands of brilliant color began streaking the sky. The sun was setting and it was gorgeous. Despite Philip's fatigue and hunger, he could not help but admire the singular beauty of the sight. Vibrant shades of purple, yellow, orange, and red – it looked as if God himself was painting the vast expanse above Philip's head in real time, the clouds and sky a massive canvas for His experiments in Impressionism.

"I could learn to like it out here." Philip was developing an affinity for the desert.

When Philip's astonishment subsided, the inevitability of the approaching nightfall became real for him. The heat of the day had been replaced by a distinct chill in the air. The rapid and extreme drop in temperature surprised and frightened Philip. He frantically began to look for a place to spend the night. "I don't think I'll be doing much sleeping tonight," he said. Still, he needed to find a spot which would provide him with a semblance of security.

Not far ahead, he spotted a tree silhouetted against the darkening sky. He had only seen a small number of them all day – they were few and far between on the desert plains. Though thin, spindly, and rather insubstantial, the tree had sufficient vegetation to provide a little cover and, most importantly, the sensation of safety.

Philip covered the short distance to the tree in a spirited trot. He cleared a spot at the base of the tree and sat down with his back to its trunk. The sun had now fully set, the brilliant colors of a few short minutes prior drained from the sky, leaving only inky dark blue and the vague forms of shifting clouds.

Philip pulled his knees up to his chest and shivered. He made a valiant effort to keep his mind from imagining all the potential dangers that might have been lurking in the dark. He was only nominally successful. Visions of snakes, scorpions, and venomous lizards filled his head like unwanted intruders. "It's going to be a long night," Philip sighed. He put his head in his folded arms and closed his eyes...then promptly fell fast asleep. Exhaustion, total and debilitating, had overridden his fear. His body and mind rested.

In the middle of the night, Philip awoke with a start.

Something was moving in the dark – something big, something breathing heavily...something *close*. Philip stood up immediately, ready to defend himself. His body became a taut wire coursing with electricity. His brain was on fire, ignited by pure, primal instinct.

Philip strained his eyes in the darkness, trying to catch a glimpse of the large form that lurked somewhere just beyond the tree, his tiny oasis of safety. The dark was impenetrable. The landscape and its inhabitants were fully cloaked in the thick veil of the moonless night. Philip could still hear the creature. It seemed to be circling the tree at a fair distance – too far to be seen, but close enough for its threatening presence to be felt. Philip could even hear the...*thing*...moaning in a low, guttural voice that sounded neither human nor animal. *What* is *that*? Philip thought.

Remaining as still and silent as he could, Philip struggled to stay calm. He was on the verge of panicking...and he knew it. He had the sudden and irrational urge to run. *That would be stupid*, he reminded himself. *That thing is waiting for you to make a move.*

The creature in the darkness continued to pace and circle Philip's position. Philip's fear grew until it eventually got the better of him. He picked up a large branch and, before he was fully aware of what he was doing, jumped to his feet and yelled out, "What do you want?! I'll kill you! Go away!"

Silence followed. Philip stood in a combat stance, ready to use the branch as a weapon on whatever was out there apparently stalking him. Nothing happened. *Did I scare it away?* It seemed highly unlikely, yet the night was once again still and quiet. Philip stood there for what seemed like an eternity, unwilling to relax his guard and trust the deceptive, eerie calm that had returned to the desert.

Minutes passed and nothing happened. Philip returned to a sitting position at the base of the tree, but kept his grip firm on the stick. There would be no more sleep for him on this night. He waited for the sun to rise. Many hours later, it did. Deep crimson light seeped into the desert and spread across the sky in a resplendent display. Even in his nervous, sleepless state, Philip was able to admire the magnificent morning vista. He considered his next move.

When Philip stood up to stretch, he again became aware of the metal object lodged in his spine. He poked at it tentatively. There was no pain, just the uncomfortable sensation of something alien inhabiting his body. "Someone's going to answer for this," he muttered. "I will find you and make you pay."

Philip began to survey the area around the tree, looking for any sign of the thing that he had heard in the middle of the night. He found something much stranger than what he had expected. Ten feet or so from where he had sat all night under the tree lay an object. It had not been there the night before, Philip was sure of that. Philip approached it cautiously.

The object was an oblong box about a foot long, six inches wide, and four inches tall. Philip reached into his pocket and retrieved the smaller one he had found the day before. The boxes were of different sizes, but of similar design. Before satisfying his curiosity about what the new box might contain, Philip swallowed a pill from the vial resting in the small box. The tablets apparently worked – he did not feel any symptoms of dehydration.

Philip inhaled deeply, bent down and released the metal clasp of the new box, then opened the lid. It contained two items – a small foil-wrapped energy bar and what appeared to be a strange, hand-held power tool. "Must be a care package from my secret admirer," Philip said. His stomach began to rumble as soon as he spotted the energy bar. He tore open the wrapper and gobbled up the vaguely chocolate-flavored confection in three ravenous bites. He could instantly feel warmth and strength spreading through his body.

Next, Philip carefully removed the strange tool. It was like a futuristic cross between a flashlight and a handgun and totally unlike anything he had ever seen before. There was a button on its underside just above the formed grip. The business end of the thing had the flared appearance of a musket barrel. It was like a prop from a low-budget science fiction movie. "What *is* this thing?" Philip wondered. He pointed it at a large boulder. He was about to push the button – the trigger – but uncertainty caused him to pause.

"Fuck it." Philip pushed the button. He braced himself for anything – a gunshot, an explosion, a laser burst, a shockwave, the complete obliteration of the boulder in a flash of lightning...but instead, the 'tool' emitted a faint beam of light which made the boulder appear purple in its glow. "Weird," Philip said. He slid the object into one of his capacious pockets.

Philip was about to walk on and leave the box behind when he noticed something else resting inside. It was another note. He picked it up. It said: *Use this tool in case of an emergency. Aim at your target and push the button. Has an effective range of 100 feet.* "Okay, then." Philip was skeptical, but intrigued. "I'll remember that. Thank you."

Feeling somewhat rejuvenated, Philip moved on, away from the tree and toward his destination in the mountains – toward whatever mysteriously awaited him at the location indicated by the star on the map.

By the time the sun was once again nearing its midday point in the sky, Philip had made great progress. The mountains loomed above him now, practically within striking distance. He was close enough to see faint trails snaking their way through the valleys and up the peaks. Using the map and his apparent position to estimate how much ground he had already covered, Philip calculated that he had traveled approximately halfway from where he had begun his long, arduous, involuntary trek to the mountain location where he hoped to find rest...and answers.

Awareness of how far he had come and how close he was to what could potentially be the end of his lonely and frightening sojourn in the desert filled him with renewed determination. "If I can get into the mountains by nightfall," he said, "I should be able to reach the star tomorrow afternoon." He had no idea what he would find and had no desire to speculate.

Soon, he was at the foot of the closest mountain – a fair-sized formation with a moderate slope. Ascending would not be as difficult nor as treacherous as Philip had anticipated. There appeared to be trails leading all the way up.

Philip pushed his way through some thorny bushes, probing for a trailhead. He was focused on the ground and vegetation directly in his path and did not see the figure hiding in the bushes mere feet from where he stood until he was almost right on top of it. When he did spot the shape of a man crouching in the thick bush, he let out a shocked cry and jumped back. Wide, startled eyes peered at him from the shadows. Philip stared back in horror. The eyes belonged to an individual who looked more like an animal than a human being. Long, matted hair framed a filth-encrusted face, giving the man the distinct look of an anthropological throwback. The crouching savage bared his black, rotten teeth in a feral expression of intimidation.

"Whoa, there," Philip said, raising his hands slowly in a gesture of peaceful intention. "I'm not going to hurt you."

The man in the bushes started to rise, his eyes still

locked on Philip's. He growled menacingly through clenched and exposed teeth. Philip lowered his right hand to his hip, where the strange apparatus was resting in his pocket. His fingers found their way to the implement – or weapon, as he had been informed of in the note – and closed around it.

The man in the bushes raised his thin, sinewy arms and clawed his hands up in front of him in a provocative, threatening manner. Philip could sense an attack coming. He had to act *now*...so he did. He pulled out the lightgun, aimed it at the feral man, and pushed the button, hoping for the best. Just as when he had tested the item on the boulder, the strange tool silently emitted a beam of light, illuminating the snarling, sneering, attacker in a weird shade of purple. The man in the bushes froze, confused.

"Bang, bang," Philip joked. "Gotcha."

Before either of them could make a move, Philip saw something extremely unsettling. Behind and above the savage in the bushes, he could see throbbing, translucent, amorphous blobs floating in the air around the man's head. The shapes moved like jellyfish in water, flitting, undulating, and dancing about. The man in the bushes seemed to be entirely unaware of them. Philip then realized that the light of the device he held in his hand had exposed the bizarre entities.

"Looks like you've got bigger trouble than me, my friend," Philip said, gesturing at the creatures floating in the air around the man's head. The man seemed to understand – his posture relaxed and he looked in the direction Philip was indicating. Philip kept the light trained on the creatures. When the man spotted them, they suddenly scattered, as if aware of being seen. The otherworldly entities dispersed in all directions and disappeared. The two men observed the uncanny event in stunned silence.

When the man in the bushes returned his gaze to

Philip, Philip was amazed to see that a transformation had taken place. Though still dirty, disheveled, and nearly naked, a spark of intelligence and a sheen of total awareness had replaced the wild, mad look in the man's eyes. His jaw had also loosened and his teeth were no longer clenched. Philip was even more astounded when the man spoke. "What just happened?" the man in the bushes asked. "Who are *you*?"

Philip extended his hand. "I'm Philip, and I think we just said goodbye to some of your invisible friends."

The man in the bushes grasped Philip's hand and shook it firmly and sincerely. "My name is Charlie. Thank you for...your help."

Charlie rubbed his eyes and took a series of deep breaths. "I feel like I've been sleepwalking for a century," he said, "or like I just woke up from a very long and vivid nightmare."

Charlie surveyed their position. "Where did you come from?"

"I wish I had a good answer for you. I woke up in the desert yesterday morning. I have no memory. Some weird shit happened. I found out that my name is Philip. I started walking. Spent the night alone under a tree. More weird shit happened. Walked some more until I found you and..."

"Some *really* weird shit happened," Charlie finished the sentence for him.

"Indeed," Philip smiled.

Philip noticed that he and Charlie were wearing practically identical clothes, although Charlie's T-shirt and shorts were stained, tattered, and nearly falling apart. It was a major clue that the two men had endured similar ordeals.

"I don't suppose you happen to have a map, do you?" Philip took a guess.

"Yes, I do, as a matter of fact." Charlie reached into his pocket. He pulled out a piece of paper as torn and tattered as his clothing. Philip retrieved his map and compared it to Charlie's. They were identical, complete with the same star indicating a location somewhere in the mountains Philip had been about to explore. The star near the bottom of Charlie's map, however, was far to the east of Philip's starting location.

"Isn't that interesting," Philip said.

"What do you suppose it *means*?" Charlie asked. "Why *us*? Who's responsible?" He was fully cognizant of the fact that neither of the men had any clue what they were doing or what was happening, but he couldn't help vocalizing his profound confusion.

"I think if we make our way to that location on the map, we may find some answers. That's about all I'm sure of right now. Care to join me?"

"You're the one packing the heat," Charlie joked. "I don't have a ghostbusting flashlight like you do. It would be in my best interest to stay close...plus, you may have saved my life. Thank you, again, for that."

"To be honest, I had no idea what this thing is or what it could do. I just kinda acted on instinct. I thought you were going to tear my throat out."

"It really was like being in a dream," Charlie recalled. "I have vague memories of wandering through the desert like a drugged-up zombie, trying to crawl back to reality from the depths of a deep, black pit for how long, I have no idea."

"Are you thirsty or hungry?"

"Surprisingly, not really."

Charlie put a hand in his pocket and pulled out a bottle of hydration tablets. It was half empty. Digging further, he found empty energy bar wrappers. "Somehow I had the presence of mind to keep my body sustained," he said.

"Those things were feeding on you," Philip said. It was a leap of insight, but when he spoke, he knew it to be true. "Feeding on your energy – on your lifeforce. I'm sure they needed you alive and at least *physically* healthy."

"Parasites..." Charlie shivered, "invisible fucking parasites...Just when I thought it couldn't get any weirder."

"It can *always* get weirder."

Philip and Charlie bushwhacked their way out of the tangled underbrush and began to ascend the mountain. After a short but tricky scramble over rocks and around various species of flora of the extremely spiky and painful variety, they reached a well-worn trail that appeared to wind up and around the mountain.

After taking a moment to catch his breath and examine the map, Philip said, "This looks promising. Let's stay on the trail for as long as we can. We should keep going until we find a safe place to spend the night. I think we can reach the star on the map sometime tomorrow afternoon if we make good progress early."

Charlie was winded, but managed to nod in agreement. "Let's do it," he sputtered. The two men moved on.

They had been hiking for about an hour, each man quietly content with his own thoughts, when Charlie spotted something ahead. "Check it out," he said. "A sign."

"I see it."

There was indeed a sign, planted at what seemed to be a fork in the path.

"Looks like a trail marker to me," Philip said.

The two hikers approached the sign. It was a piece of thin, rectangular metal attached to a sturdy post in the ground, but Philip was wrong – it did not indicate which trail they were on, but instead had three simple words embossed on its glossy surface: *SURVIVORS THIS WAY.* An arrow next to the message pointed to the trail leading right – a trail that would take them to the summit of the mountain.

Philip was in the lead as they made their final ascent and was the first to crest the mountain. Charlie was still climbing when he saw Philip freeze at the peak. Philip stood motionless and gazed out at the valley below with a look of utter astonishment on his face.

"Is everything okay?" Charlie asked.

"I can't believe it," Philip said, shaking his head incredulously.

"What *is* it?!" Charlie cried as he sprinted the last few feet to stand at Philip's side. When he reached the summit, he was too stunned to speak and simply gawked at the sight before him with his mouth agape.

From their vantage point at the apex, Philip and Charlie had a clear view of the entire valley, a wide basin which stretched for miles between where they stood and a distant range of mountains far to the north. To the south, the vast expanse of the desert they had spent the last two days crossing was visible. The panorama was spectacular.

What was most incredible, however, was what they could now see spread out on the valley floor in front of them – the ruins of a very large and completely demolished city. It lay cradled among the peaks like the carcass of some long dead and desiccated beast. The totality of the destruction was practically incomprehensible. There were vast swaths in which nothing remained – the structures which once stood in those areas had been completely razed, leaving large pockets of scorched earth. The skeletal remains of the downtown core jutted out of the center of the destroyed city. High-rise towers poked up from the rubble like cracked and sun-bleached ribs. There was no light, no movement, and no sign of life.

"Holy shit," Charlie finally said.

"You took the words right out of my mouth," Philip said.

"Earthquake? Nukes? Meteor?"

"I haven't got a clue, but it sure looks like the wrath of God to me."

The sun was beginning to set. The golden hour had come, painting the mountains on the far side of the valley in warm, brilliant shades of orange and casting deep, ominous shadows on the ruins of the city below. Philip was about to suggest that they move on and find a place to spend the night when he noticed that Charlie was idle, staring into space with a spooky, vacant expression on his face.

"Hey, are you okay?" Philip asked with sudden concern. Charlie did not respond.

"*Charlie!*" Philip yelled. He grasped Charlie's shoulders and gave him a vigorous shaking. "Charlie! Snap out of it!"

As he attempted to communicate with Charlie, Philip began to experience an unpleasant sensation in his head – a distressing buzzing sound accompanied by tendrils of pain which wiggled their way deep into his brain. He began to lose his ability to think clearly and could actually feel his consciousness fading away.

Philip marshaled the force of his will. He was able to retain enough control to reach a hand into the pocket where the lightgun rested. As if from a third-person perspective, he observed himself pulling the weapon out and pointing it at the apparently empty space between Charlie and himself. He pushed the button, instantly revealing the invisible parasites that had gathered in the air around them. The creatures pulsated in the purple light as they fed.

Philip struggled for control of his mind. *Leave us alone*, he thought. *Go back to Hell*. The command worked. The parasites abruptly scattered. Philip's tenuous tether to reality snapped back. He was plugged back in, restored – fully aware and in control once again. Charlie, too, had recovered.

"Those things were sucking on me again, weren't they?" Charlie asked rhetorically.

"We have to be very careful. Those things are nasty, insidious little bastards. I think they are attracted to intense emotion – fear, anger, despair. We need to watch ourselves. Try to stay calm, cool, and collected."

Looking down upon the ruined city was disturbing. Philip and Charlie had a strong desire to move on and leave the shattered corpse of civilization behind. The path indicated by the *SURVIVORS THIS WAY* sign they had passed continued along a ridge that connected the peak on which they stood with a series of others that wrapped around the valley. Philip and Charlie proceeded up the trail in the dwindling light.

"Let's get as far away as possible from that city," Charlie said. *Maybe it's haunted*, he thought. *Maybe those things floating in the air are ghosts...*

Philip pointed to the farthest peak in sight. It was silhouetted black against the deepening twilight. "I think we can reach that hill in a few hours," he estimated. "We can rest there and move out first thing in the morning."

The mountains were fully submerged in darkness when Philip and Charlie made the decision to stop and rest for the night. For the last two hours, they had hiked the ridge with near zero visibility. Philip had occasionally used the lightgun to check for and ward off parasites, but with no knowledge of the item's power supply or charge, he had used it sparingly.

The various enigmatic dangers that lurked in the murky, blue-black gloom had remained concealed. The mountains had so far granted them safe passage. The hikers arrived at a plateau just off the trail – it was just large enough for the two men to lie down in. Philip and Charlie each cleared a small patch of ground and stretched out.

"I don't know if *I'll* be getting any sleep tonight," Charlie said as he struggled to find a comfortable position on the hard ground.

"Just close your eyes and rest," Philip suggested.

"Easier said then done," Charlie retorted. Ironically, he was asleep in seconds. His mind and body had reached their limit.

Philip lay awake, listening to Charlie snore and searching his mind for any clue to his own identity. Incomplete, fleeting memories taunted him from just beyond his recollection. Indistinct scenes formed in the deep recesses of his subconscious but never broke the surface. Tantalizing clues, fuzzy images, snippets of conversation, and random sensory impressions lingered on the outer perimeter of his awareness – so close, yet agonizingly out of reach.

Before Philip drifted off to sleep, he used the lightgun once more to sweep the immediate area for parasites. Finding none, he settled back and allowed himself to slip into unconsciousness. The two men slept side by side on the mountain. In the valley below, the shattered remnants of the city lay silent and barren in its final repose.

Philip and Charlie awoke as the first rays of the sun appeared on the horizon and began to spread over the valley and the mountains. The two men were sore, stiff, and groggy, but rested and ready for the day ahead.

"Not exactly luxury accommodations," Charlie smirked, "but at least I was able to sleep."

"Good. You'll need your strength for – " He stopped mid-sentence as he spotted something sitting at the edge of the clearing – it was another box. It was resting on the ground where they had stepped off the trail.

Charlie followed Philip's gaze and saw it too. "Was that there last night?"

"I don't think so," Philip said as he walked over to the box. "I'm sure one of us would have seen it."

"It was dark when we got here."

"True, but look at the size of it."

The box was much larger than the others they had found on their journey. It was knee-high and nearly three feet across. It very much resembled a footlocker. Philip crouched down, released the metal clasp, and opened it.

The box was full of supplies: new clothes, new shoes, boxes of energy bars, two backpacks, another lightgun, and even two large canteens full of water.

"Wow!" Charlie cried when he saw the contents. "The motherlode!"

"Someone is apparently looking out for us," Philip said.

"Our guardian angel," Charlie mused.

"Something like that."

Charlie immediately stripped down and began changing. The new clothes were identical to what he had been wearing: simple white T-shirts, cargo shorts, and rugged hiking shoes. The clothes Philip had been wearing were nowhere near as dirty and tattered as Charlie's, but he, too, changed. It felt good.

Each man then chose a canteen and a backpack. They filled the backpacks with energy bars and slung them over their shoulders.

"I assume this is for me," Charlie said, picking up the second lightgun.

The large box was now empty, revealing a neatly folded piece of paper at the bottom. "Another note from our anonymous benefactor," Philip said. He plucked it out of the box and read it out loud:

"Congratulations on making it this far! It is a remarkable accomplishment. Here are some supplies to help you on the final leg of your journey. Your ordeal has almost reached its conclusion, but there are still challenges ahead. Stay alert, stay vigilant, stay strong. We look forward to seeing you when you arrive."

The note was not signed. Philip and Charlie contemplated the mysterious message.

"Well, that's intriguing," Charlie said, "and totally baffling."

"Leaves me with more questions than answers," Philip said.

The two men stepped onto the trail and began walking. They continued to hike in the direction indicated by the sign they had passed the day before. From their current position, the path rose and fell over a series of small mountains, culminating on a high peak barely visible in the hazy morning light.

"I think our destination is the valley beyond that last peak," Philip said as he compared his map to the terrain in front of them.

"That's not so bad," Charlie said. "I bet we can get there by early afternoon."

The hikers fell into their rhythm. Hearts pumping, legs working, eyes scanning, minds relaxing into an introspective drift, they slipped into a state of automatic locomotion. They hiked in comfortable silence. The sun rose in the sky as they made progress, bathing them in warmth and light.

They had been walking along for a few hours when Philip, who had been in the lead as usual, stopped suddenly and gasped. The section of trail ran along a ridge that dropped off steeply to one side. "Oh, no..." Philip said, "look." He was pointing to something far below the sharp cliff.

Charlie walked to the rocky edge carefully and peered down. He, too, gasped. There was a body down there, smashed against the rocks and burst open in awful shades of black, purple, and red that contrasted highly with the gray stones. The body was bloated and partly devoured by scavengers. It had apparently been there for quite some time.

"That's disgusting," Charlie said.

"Poor soul," Philip said. "He must have fallen."

It was a terrible sight, more sad than frightening. Philip and Charlie looked down upon the body in solemn reflection, suddenly acutely aware of their own mortality.

"There's nothing we can do for him," Philip said. "Trying to get down there to bury him would be too dangerous. We might end up in the same condition. We'll have to leave him."

"Hey, check it out!" Charlie exclaimed. He had spotted something on the other side of the trail, partially hidden in a creosote bush. "It's a backpack," he said as he pulled it free.

"It must have belonged to the dead man," Philip said. "Open it."

"Someone already did," Charlie observed. "It's empty."

The backpack had been torn wide open and ransacked. There was nothing inside but a few empty energy bar wrappers.

"I have a bad feeling that guy was robbed," Philip said, "...and killed."

"Maybe it was an animal..."

"I doubt it." Philip couldn't be certain, of course, but his intuition was strong.

"Let's get out of here," Charlie said. "I'm freaked out."

Philip and Charlie left the empty backpack and the

deceased man just as they had found them and moved on. After a few minutes of hiking, they came to a curve in the trail that took them around the mountain. When they got to the other side of the bend, they were again presented with a strange and unexpected sight.

At the side of the trail a few yards from where Philip and Charlie had rounded the bend stood a crude sign, propped up by a pile of rocks. It seemed to mark the entrance to a cave – or perhaps a mine – carved into the side of the mountain. The opening appeared to be illuminated by the light of a fire inside. Shadows danced on the walls of the cave and on the trail in front. Philip and Charlie could hear faint voices emanating from within.

"Be careful," Philip whispered. "Go slowly, quietly." He was spooked and more than a little concerned.

"Does that cave match up to where the star is on the map?" Charlie asked in hushed excitement.

"I don't think so. Doesn't seem like we've gone far enough yet."

"Listen...there are people in there! I bet they're the ones we were supposed to find!" Charlie was insistent as he moved forward.

"Be careful!" Philip hissed.

Charlie approached the sign. "This is it!" he mouthed.

Philip crept up to the sign. It said: *SURVIVORS HERE.* The words were barely legible and had been scrawled on a rough piece of wood with what appeared to be mud...or blood.

"I don't know," Philip whispered. "I think we should keep going." Philip nodded toward the mountain up ahead. The trail continued past the cave and meandered over more rolling hills before the final visible peak. "I have a bad feeling about this place," Philip said. "Let's get out of here."

The voices in the cave suddenly ceased. Philip and

Charlie froze. The fire flickered in the mouth of the cave. After a few moments of intense silence, sounds of scuffling issued forth from somewhere deep within the rock walls.

"We should run," Philip urged. It was too late. A man appeared. He stepped out of the cave and stood on the trail directly in front of Philip and Charlie.

"Greetings, travelers!" the man exclaimed in a booming, cheerful voice. "Welcome!"

The man was extremely tall and robust. On his large, powerful frame, he wore a flowing white robe. His beard was thick and bushy. His hair was long and brown. His eyes sparkled with compassion, humor, and intelligence. He carried a large, hand-carved, wooden staff.

"My name is Ezekiel," the robed man said. "I'm so glad you found us. Please, won't you join us in our humble abode for a warm meal? You must be exhausted." Ezekiel's radiant grin was disarming.

"I'm Charlie, and this is Philip!" Charlie's enthusiasm was obvious. "We're so glad we finally made it. We saw a dead man back there. Poor guy...he was so close..."

Philip remained silent.

"Yes, it's unfortunate," Ezekiel frowned. "Not all who seek will find. Not all travelers reach their destination. Now, please, come inside. Meet the others." Ezekiel motioned toward the cave opening with an exaggerated sweep of his arm.

Charlie needed no more encouragement. He stepped into the cave. Philip hung back, reticent.

"I know you have a lot of questions, Philip," Ezekiel said. "I can help you find answers."

"Have you ever seen one of these?" Philip asked as he drew the lightgun from his pocket.

"Of course I have," Ezekiel said. "I helped design it."

Philip gave Ezekiel a quizzical look. "I see..." he said.

"Then you won't mind if I use it. No disrespect intended, of course...it's just that we've had some scares. Better safe than sorry, right?"

"Right, indeed," Ezekiel replied with a smile. "By all means, use the item as you wish. When you are satisfied that we offer no threat, please join us by the fire for refreshments."

Ezekiel ducked into the cave. Philip pushed the button on the lightgun and kept it directed in front of him as he cautiously followed Ezekiel through the opening. Philip scanned the room as he entered, using both his eyes and the lightgun.

The interior of the cave was brightly lit, surprisingly commodious, and full of people and objects. There was a stone pit in the center of the cave containing a rather large fire. Around it, a group of ten or more people were sitting and talking quietly. There were tables, desks, and strange apparatus throughout the expansive interior, which stretched farther back than could be seen. Deeper in, people were milling about, involved in a variety of tasks. No one seemed to notice Ezekiel, Charlie, or Philip. Philip aimed the lightgun in all directions and could find no parasites.

"You're safe here," Ezekiel said. "You don't need that item any more. This is a perfectly clean environment. We have taken steps to ensure that those...*things*...won't survive in here."

"How did you manage that?" Philip asked.

"All in due time, my friend," Ezekiel replied. "All your questions will be answered, I assure you."

"This place is *amazing!*" Charlie cried. "Look at all this *stuff!*"

"Would you care for something to eat? A warm beverage, perhaps?"

"Sure!" Charlie said.

"Jennifer, could you get these gentlemen some tea and biscuits, please?" Ezekiel addressed a young woman who was operating a strange device in a corner of the cave. It appeared to be equipment used in the preparation of food.

"Of course!" Jennifer promptly replied as she manipulated some knobs and pushed a few buttons. Hot liquid began pouring from a spout on the unusual device and Jennifer collected it in cups. A small door opened and out popped fresh biscuits. Jennifer gathered them on a plate and brought the snacks and drinks to where Ezekiel stood with Philip and Charlie.

"Welcome!" Jennifer greeted them genially. "It's always nice to see new faces. I hope your travels weren't too difficult. Enjoy these delicious snacks!" Her smile radiated warmth and hospitality.

"Thank you, Jennifer," Ezekiel said. "I was just about to introduce Philip and Charlie to the family and show them around."

"Oh!" Jennifer cried. "You're going to *love* it here. We *are* a family. I'm so delighted you two survived and found us!"

"All these people are survivors?" Philip asked.

"Yes," Ezekiel replied. "Just like you."

"What *happened*?" Charlie asked. "What happened to the world? Why can't we remember anything?"

"Come, sit with me," Ezekiel said. He led Philip and Charlie to the fire. The assembled crowd shifted, providing the threesome with a bare patch of floor on which to sit. There were men and women in the group, all wearing identical robes – light brown, not the pure white of Ezekiel's, as though of lower rank. Conspicuously, there were no children present. Once Ezekiel and the new arrivals were seated among them, the group sat in hushed reverence.

"Hello, brothers and sisters," Ezekiel said.

"Hello, Brother Ezekiel," the group said in unison.

"Please welcome Philip and Charlie."

"Welcome, Philip and Charlie!" the group cheered.

"Hello," Charlie smiled, "and thank you so much. It's so wonderful to be here."

"Hi," Philip said.

"We truly hope you enjoy your stay here," Ezekiel said. "We would love for you to join us – to join our family."

"Great," Charlie was now grinning widely. "That sounds just great."

"So, who exactly *are* you people?" Philip asked. "And where did you get all this...*stuff?*"

"We are, quite simply, the inheritors of the planet," Ezekiel said. "We are the architects and inhabitants of the New World. We have been chosen to lead mankind into the future – to pick up the fractured and scattered pieces of our species and repopulate this devastated planet."

"Where did all this equipment come from?" Charlie asked in awe.

"Some of it was scavenged, some we built ourselves," Ezekiel explained. "Much was destroyed in the cataclysm, but not everything."

"How were you able to do *that?*" Philip probed. "When I woke up, I couldn't even remember my name."

"Some of us have been awake for a long time," Ezekiel replied, "and I...well, I had one distinct advantage over the other survivors."

"What *kind* of advantage?" Philip continued prodding.

"I woke up with total recall," Ezekiel stated flatly. "I had full recollection of who I had been before the destruction. My memories and skills were intact. It made me the logical candidate for a leadership position."

"I can see how that would give you quite an edge," Philip said.

"Yes, but it was imperative that I not make the same mistakes as the leaders of the old system. You have seen for yourself what *they* did to this world." For the first time, a hint of something less than pure, loving benevolence crept into Ezekiel's voice. His contempt for those who had held power in the old world was evident.

The people gathered around the fire were enthralled, hanging on each and every word that flowed from Ezekiel's mouth. Those who had been occupied in other tasks around the cave also began to congregate around the fire to listen. It was clear that Ezekiel had their complete and utter devotion.

"Naturally, other survivors were drawn to me like moths to the flame," Ezekiel said. "Like the two of you, they too had been given some basic supplies and a few vague hints on where to head upon awakening...totally inadequate, as you have seen. Whoever created this ridiculous, nonsensical, demeaning little *game* is nothing but a sick, cruel, and vindictive monster. A warped and sadistic tyrant with the mentality of a disturbed child who enjoys torturing small animals." Ezekiel's face had turned bright red and traces of froth had formed in the corners of his mouth. He was now visibly agitated and furiously indignant.

"Please excuse my anger," Ezekiel said as he calmed himself with a deep breath. "When I think about the horrors that have been inflicted upon innocent human beings, I get extremely upset."

"That's understandable," Charlie said.

"So, who exactly *were* you before the shit hit the fan?" Philip asked.

Ezekiel smiled. "Before the...*cataclysm*, I worked in the technology sector, which is how I knew how to re-purpose and reprogram all of this old equipment you see in here." Throughout the cave, on every available surface, were banks of computers of all makes and models and monitors of all sizes. There was an astonishingly wide variety of laptops, tablets, and hand-held devices scattered everywhere. Amazingly, most appeared to be operational.

"You have *electricity* in here?" Philip was skeptical.

"We have a source of power," Ezekiel said. "Once you have settled in and worked with us for a while, you will understand more."

"What do you *do* with all this stuff?" Charlie asked.

"As I mentioned, we are preparing to re-establish civilization. This time, however, it will be in *our* image, of *our* design – far superior to the failed attempts of those who drove mankind to the precipice, to the very brink of extinction. We can – and will – do much better."

The crowd of robed followers had remained silent up to this moment, but upon hearing Ezekiel's proclamation, they erupted in joyous cheers.

"We are united by our singular goal," Ezekiel continued. "We have one purpose. We are, as it were, of one mind."

"Amazing," Charlie gushed. "It's just incredible what you guys have been able to accomplish. This place is awesome. It really is."

"One mind," Philip said. "Kind of like a – what's that term? – *hive* mind?"

"Yes, that's an accurate analogy," Ezekiel nodded. "We are all focused on the same task. We all have the same desires, the same goals, the same vision for the future. United, nothing can stand in our way."

"Am I to assume that if we stay, we can work toward this goal of yours?" Philip made no effort to disguise his incredulity. "We, too, can become of 'one mind' with you and the others?"

"Of course!"Ezekiel exclaimed. "By surviving and successfully reaching your destination, you have earned the right to join us in the New World. We would love to have you."

"That would be so cool," Charlie said. "I think I'd really like that."

"You will also have the exciting opportunity to assist me as I continue the work I began before the destruction," Ezekiel said.

"What exactly were you working on?" Philip inquired.

"Genetics, nanotech, robotics – fairly mainstream, mundane stuff...until I had my greatest breakthrough..." Ezekiel trailed off, unable – or unwilling – to share a deep secret.

"You see, the world simply wasn't ready to accept what I had to offer," Ezekiel continued, "but now the time has come. Humanity is ready for the greatest gift of all."

"What exactly are we talking about here?" Philip pushed for more information.

"Immortality, of course," Ezekiel said. "We have reached the singularity."

Philip processed what he had just heard. "Are you saying that you have developed some kind of technology that will allow people to live forever?"

"Yes, we have defeated death," Ezekiel replied.

"Wow, that's *amazing!*" Charlie was enchanted.

"You have survived the tribulation and you have earned your reward," Ezekiel said. "Your spinal implant, have you wondered about its purpose?"

"It crosses my mind from time to time," Philip admitted.

"I was part of the design team," Ezekiel said. "It is a marvelous invention. It is an RF receiver that allows direct access to all systems – bloodstream, endocrine, muscles, brain...we can even alter the body on a genetic level. All of this is done using a computer interface."

"That's impressive...and frightening," Philip said.

"Not at all," Ezekiel said. "Look at the people around you. They have all received their upgrades. Do they not seem perfectly happy and extraordinarily healthy?"

The assembled crowd murmured in agreement. Philip's eyes passed over them, and each individual was ostensibly fit and content.

"Sign me up and plug me in!" Charlie blurted.

"That's the spirit, Charlie," Ezekiel grinned. "We can start your upgrades immediately, if you'd like."

"Sure, that would be cool!" Charlie said.

"Are you sure you want to go through with that?" Philip asked. "Seems so intrusive and risky..."

"There is no risk whatsoever," Ezekiel said. "The technology has been rigorously tested and perfected."

"They are survivors...like us," Charlie said. "We can trust them."

"Charlie, just give it a little thought. You don't have to rush into it..." Philip insisted.

"I'm really hungry, really sore, and really tired," Charlie said. "The machine will fix me."

"Yes, Charlie, it will," Ezekiel said . "You'll never feel pain or discomfort again, actually."

"See? Doesn't that sound *awesome*?" Charlie was practically begging to be jacked in.

"Jennifer, would you care to assist Charlie? He is ready for his upgrades."

Jennifer approached Charlie and held out her hand. "If you'd like to come with me, we can begin the process," she said.

"Cool," Charlie said as he grasped her hand and stood

up.

Philip stood, too, and put a hand on Charlie's shoulder. "Please, Charlie," he said, "just think it over a little bit. You might regret this."

"It is wrong to hinder the development of another person." Ezekiel was getting irritated. "To be quite honest, it is also foolish to stand in the way of evolution. Charlie is an adult. He can think and act for himself, and I believe he has made his decision."

"Yeah," Charlie said. "It's okay. I want to do this. I think these guys have a good thing here. I want to be part of the New World."

"It's a painless procedure," Ezekiel said. "You won't even notice the RF transmission and, when it's over, you're going to feel like a new man. You'll still be *you*, of course, only improved."

Philip's intuition was sending out a multitude of warning signals. Though he couldn't put his finger directly on it, or even attempt to articulate it, there was something disturbing, unnatural, and perhaps even evil about what was happening in the cave. Ezekiel, his followers, and their plethora of weird technology spooked him on a visceral level. He decided to get out of there as quickly as he could.

"You've made up your mind, Charlie, and I respect that," Philip said, "but if it's okay with you and everyone else, I think I'll be leaving now. I'm feeling a little claustrophobic...and I'm kind of a loner anyway."

Philip got up and moved toward the mouth of the cave. "Thank you so much for your hospitality," he said. "The snacks were delicious..."

Before Philip could step out of the cave and get back onto the trail, the robed congregation quickly rose and surrounded him in a synchronized, fluid swarm.

"I'm afraid I must insist that you stay," Ezekiel said from behind the wall of minions.

The small army of automaton acolytes began to close in on Philip, tightening the circle around him in a preternaturally coordinated maneuver. He was running out of options. The window of opportunity for escaping was quickly closing.

"I can sense your fear," Ezekiel said. "So very human...and so very obsolete. We are the future. Don't you see that? Your emotions have clouded your reason."

"Get back," Philip said to the mob. He raised his fists and assumed a boxer's stance. He was prepared to defend himself. "I'm warning you...get the fuck away from me!"

Ezekiel laughed. "Such aggression! Look at this atavistic throwback. You, Philip, represent everything rotten and filthy in human nature. Individualism, bravado, stubborn attachment to outmoded ideals...let go of the past. Let go of your regressive tendencies. Embrace evolution or perish."

The crowd of drones stood silently, all eyes locked on Philip. Someone near the back of the cave now spoke. It was Charlie. "It's wonderful, Philip," he smiled. "I feel like a new man." The procedure was over. Charlie had been assimilated.

"Stop fighting and join us," Charlie urged as he merged with the mob that had surrounded Philip.

Philip's intuition was practically screaming: *get away NOW!* He could not directly account for his intense aversion to what was happening in the cave – he was simply repulsed by Ezekiel and his people, as if they represented an ancient enemy. Philip's memory had been wiped and it was as though he recognized the opposition on a subconscious – or perhaps epigenetic – level.

Hands began to claw and grasp at Philip's clothing. The mob was about to subdue him. Philip reacted by swinging at the closest minion, catching the surprised man with a clean blow to the cheek. The man he struck tottered on his feet and fell back. Philip kept swinging, landing a series of punches on the people directly in his way. The robed drones were not fighters, collapsing easily under Philip's frenzied barrage. Soon, he had cleared a path to the mouth of the cave.

Ezekiel sighed as he watched the melee. "Philip, you are a fool. A silly, misguided, stubborn fool. You and your kind will soon be extinct. Farewell."

Philip sprinted for the exit. No one made any more attempts to stop him. Philip left the cave without looking back and began jogging up the trail. The sun was high and the heat was dry and intense. Philip ran along the rocky trail until the cave was far behind him and the last peak was within striking distance. He was so close.

Philip pushed himself to keep going. Drops of sweat fell from his face and hair in time to the rhythm of his stride. He was focused purely on reaching his destination: the top of the last visible hill. Machine-like, he drove toward it, his muscles straining, his heart beating so hard in his chest that it felt like it was about to burst. Philip did not stop or even slow down as he reached the base of the hill – he powered himself straight up its rugged incline.

At the top, Philip stopped and stood, panting. He found himself looking out upon another valley. It was a gorgeous sight – a broad, verdant basin nestled in the arid and rocky mountains that jutted from the desert floor. To Philip's utter amazement, there was a village in the valley. He could see cabins, barns, and other structures arranged neatly along rough, unpaved roads. A large patchwork of tilled fields lay adjacent to the village and stretched for many miles. Consulting the map and comparing it to the landscape he now observed before him, Philip was certain he had reached his destination – the location indicated by the star.

Upon closer inspection, Philip could see people below – men, women, and children – working in the fields and walking along the streets of the settlement. There were no cars or power lines. It was an astonishing scene – a vision of pure, untainted, idyllic beauty as rich in substance and function as it was in form and aesthetic.

A great up-welling of emotion stirred in Philip's chest as he stood quietly observing the people in the village and fields below. Tears formed in his eyes, as if the sight before him had unlocked something deep and dormant coded in his soul. He had instantly recognized the beauty and truth of what he was witnessing.

Philip's elevated vantage point on the mountain allowed him to see the larger perspective. The people of the village were living and working in harmony, co-existing with each other and with their environment. Nature had not been beaten into submission – it had been nurtured and cultivated. Work was being performed by people who cared for their families – and for the land that provided for them. Had they abandoned currency? Philip could only speculate, but he had a strong suspicion that the people who had created and maintained the little pocket of paradise were rewarded in other, more substantial ways.

Philip had been called – by whom exactly, he wasn't sure – but his ordeal was over. He had survived a great tribulation and had truly earned a place in the new community. A trail led directly from the peak where he stood down to the village. Philip set out on the final leg of his journey. He headed down the mountain and prepared to meet his destiny.

The Gamer

Gary the gamer took a large hit of Narconade and strapped on the hypno-helmet for another round. Within moments, the drug took effect and the simulation began. This particular game was his current favorite. While his body lay slumped and forgotten on a stained and tattered couch in a dimly-lit, filthy room, in his mind he was blasting undead alien enemies with a shotgun, their bulbous heads exploding in gloriously realistic ways. Gary proceeded through the intricately rendered and detailed virtual environment, firing round after round at every humanoid creature he encountered.

In the distance he spotted a temple, shimmering in the desert heat. Gary was making real progress! He had never before made it this far. His heart rate increased. He began to sweat profusely. He uttered strange, animalistic sounds under his breath and there was a certain excited stirring in his crotch. Gary was entirely unaware of his physiology – he was focused purely on reaching that temple and killing everything that stood in his way.

An exo-zombie lunged at Gary from the left...he quickly leveled his weapon and dispatched it with a blast to the face. The stirring in his groin increased. He was now fully aroused. A chuckle escaped his lips, followed closely by a long, dangling string of thick saliva. He was fast approaching the temple, an imposing stone structure vaguely Egyptian. Through the internal speakers of the helmet, he could hear faint chanting which seemed to emanate from within the temple. He could now see bizarre symbols carved into the temple's pillars.

Gary trembled in anticipation. He reduced a few more

reanimated alien corpses to green and purple piles of smoking gelatinous matter and began to ascend the steps leading up and into the inner chambers. A fierce, ominous wind swept across the desert. The chanting increased in volume and intensity. He reached the entrance to the first chamber and paused. Somewhere in the murky, hidden depths of the temple, perhaps aware of his presence and waiting in ambush, lurked the alien overlord, the ultimate foe and final target in the game.

Defeating the overlord had become an obsession for Gary. He had invested weeks, if not months, of his life on the game. Though he rarely slept, when he did, he dreamed of the alien planet. Often he could not distinguish between his dreams and his time in the hypno-helmet. He lived in a world of overlapping, amorphous realities and merged fantasies. In this moment, his consciousness was completely occupied with the task at hand – finding and killing the overlord. All other thoughts, all memories, all awareness of the 'real' world were lost to the void.

Gary took a deep, anxious breath and entered the inner sanctum. The eerie chanting suddenly ceased. It was unnaturally silent inside the temple, like the vacuum of deep space. He peered intently into the darkness with his weapon raised. He proceeded slowly, each step deliberate. Gary reached a large gallery, with tunnels leading in all directions. Nothing moved in the still gloom. Gary's entire being quivered in anticipation. Which way should he go? He could see no markings or symbols indicating the location of the overlord's chamber. He was momentarily paralyzed by indecision. His mind raced, his hands trembled. Finally he summoned the courage to move, choosing to go forward on pure instinct.

As Gary entered the far corridor, the darkness seemed to tighten around him, moving in and enveloping him in a black cloak. The hypno-helmet provided a total sensory experience and at this point he could actually smell the putrid stench of something ancient and hideous lurking in the dark. He was in a perfect state of awareness now, like a paranoid coyote slinking through the moonlight. Sweat and drool pooled at Gary's feet. He was now moaning in a low, guttural voice. He took a few more cautious steps and stopped abruptly. Movement directly ahead! A massive shape of indistinct features and proportions writhed in the shadows. He knew immediately what it was: The alien overlord was within reach! *Don't panic*, he told himself. *Don't panic!*

Gary tightened his grip on the weapon and yelled, "Come on, fucker! Bring it!" He chambered a round, preparing to fire. Nothing in his life could compare to this wonderful, glorious moment. Victory, validation, and satisfaction of the highest order were within reach. He savored the pleasure of imminent climax. What a delicious sensation! *If only real life offered such sublime experiences*, he thought. A huge smile appeared on his face.

Hoping to provoke the overlord into action, Gary started forward. He was successful. The creature suddenly lunged at him from the darkness, a shrieking, squirming mass of teeth and tentacles... Abruptly, the creature froze in midair. It hung there motionless, its shriek reverberating in Gary's ears with an unnerving staccato rhythm. The gamer attempted to fire the shotgun, but nothing happened. His virtual hands and virtual weapon were frozen in place – locked up on the helmet's view-screen.

Then he heard it – a loud, persistent banging from above his head. Gary instantly understood what was happening and it was not good. His neighbor upstairs was pounding on the floor and the ruckus had shaken loose the terminal plug by which the hypno-helmet was attached, disrupting the game. The gamer realized that his war cry must have been loud enough to upset the neighbor...it was not the first time that it had happened. Gary was absolutely mortified and sat there in shock, his mouth agape.

It took several minutes for Gary to compose himself. When he was sufficiently calm, he carefully removed the hypno-helmet and set it down on the couch beside him. He put his head in his hands, feeling defeated. He had been so close to completing the game – so close to killing the overlord and ridding that planet of alien zombies! Gary was on the verge of real tears. He had invested such a large amount of his time and energy that his sense of purpose and self-worth were intrinsically linked to the task. He whimpered and shook spasmodically. The more he thought about it, the more upset he grew. He then began to get angry.

Gary sat up, stretching his back and arms. He reached for the Narconade and finished the canister in one hit. The drug's effects were intense and immediate. His mind raced. *People are always getting in the way,* he thought. *They fuck everything up. All I've ever wanted was to be left alone to my Narconade and hypno-helmet. I'm not hurting anyone! Why are they always trying to stop me from indulging in the only things I truly enjoy in this dismal, doomed, rotten old world? Planet Earth is a shithouse. People kill each other every day over meaningless nonsense. Wars are waged on the poor, helpless, and innocent. Violence, greed, misery, and wretchedness of every variety plague this pitiful planet. Human beings are a virus.*

At least I found an escape. Gary's thoughts were spiraling out of control. *At least I have something I am passionate about. I keep to myself and cause no trouble...and they keep interfering!* His rage was increasing. *That fucking neighbor! He* knew *I was playing...probably interrupted the game on purpose! He's probably laughing about it right now.*

Fury rose in Gary's belly like sick fire. He was naturally passive and non-confrontational, but a perfect, crystalline idea entered his mind. It was suddenly clear what he must do...and he must do it NOW, before any doubt, second-guessing, or intrusive overanalysis tainted his resolve.

Gary rose from the couch. He was gaunt, emaciated, and filthy, reeking of a thousand showerless days, but he was filled with a new sense of purpose and freshly-discovered resolve. *I must kill that asshole neighbor,* he thought. It was all so clear to him now. *Retribution! Validation!* He scanned the interior of his tiny apartment, his gaze cold and intense. He spotted the perfect tool for the task – a baseball bat from his long gone childhood days in little league. He retrieved it from the corner, admiring its nicely balanced heft and enjoying its weight in his hands. Gary felt powerful again.

Clutching the bat, Gary calmly opened the door to the hall and left his apartment for the first time in days. The glare of the hallway lights surprised and stunned him, but he adjusted and made his way down the hall toward the stairway. He ascended to the next floor, now holding the bat in both hands as if approaching the plate.

Gary reached the second-level landing and was presently aware of a strange smell...a putrid, rotten stench, actually. *What kind of appalling things do these people eat? Has something died?* He gagged and felt nauseated. As he struggled to contain the contents of his stomach, the hall lights flickered. He then became aware of an eerie buzzing sound issuing from nowhere and everywhere simultaneously. Gary was starting to feel weird. For a surreal, disconcerting moment, he was not sure if he was still playing the game or not. He reached up to touch his head, but found no helmet. The hall lights blinked out and he was instantly plunged into total darkness.

Pure, primal fear fell upon Gary like a frigid wind. "What the fuck!" he yelled. "Who's there?!" He gazed into the black, straining to see down the hall and becoming ever more aware of the stench and the horrible buzzing sound. He felt like he was going crazy. He felt profoundly ill. He stood motionless, his heart racing, his body trembling. Then he saw it – something was moving in the darkness...something massive and menacing. It was moving down the hall now, and FAST. It was rushing at him, a shrieking, writhing mass of teeth and tentacles. Gary the gamer screamed as the overlord descended.

The Neighbor

<u>November 2</u> There is something strange about the new neighbor. There's something off, not quite right. To be perfectly honest, it's kind of hard to describe, but I feel it is necessary to keep a record of my concerns here, in my journal, in case my suspicions are confirmed.

The little house next door had been unoccupied for many months but a new guy just moved in. The last people to live there were a group of perfectly normal college kids who were subletting the house while attending the university. They were good kids – friendly and easy to get along with. Never caused me any trouble. I actually chilled with them at a few of their parties, which were fun. They knew how to have a good time! I got totally wasted there more than once. School finished for the year and they moved out. Not sure where they are now. I kinda miss them.

This new guy, though...I just don't know about him. He seems so *weird*. I think he's hiding something. It wouldn't surprise me if he had a really dark secret. On the day he moved in, I immediately noticed something strange. I was watching him unload his belongings from an old pickup truck, just being my usual curious self. He had boxes and boxes of stuff, all labeled: *dishes, bathroom, clothes*, etc. The weird thing is, he had a bunch of boxes labeled *books*. I mean a *lot* of 'em, like five or more full boxes. Books! That was my first clue that he was not quite normal. No one reads *books* anymore. And so many? No, I bet there was something else in those boxes.

Those boxes definitely caught my eye, so I started paying closer attention as he unloaded more stuff. Get this: at no time did I see a TV or a computer. Can you believe that?

That should tell you something right away. Something is seriously wrong with this dude! What do you think he does in his spare time? Does he read books? Ha, no. He's got to be up to some bizarre, evil stuff. Maybe he's a serial killer, or on the run from the law. Maybe he's in the witness protection program, hiding from the mob. He could be CIA, or NSA, or with some other spooky, super-secret group. Whatever it is, I'm sure it's dark and weird. You can tell just by looking at the guy.

<u>November 5</u> Just to be on the safe side, I decided to find out a little more about my mysterious new neighbor. I considered introducing myself, maybe welcoming him to the neighborhood, but that seemed too risky. If he really is hiding something, he might get suspicious if someone suddenly approached him and started asking a bunch of questions. It could totally backfire on me...plus, I was high and didn't feel like being social.

I knew I'd have to be a little more discreet, so I started watching his mail. I thought that if I could get his name, I could do some serious digging and get to the truth. Sure enough, a few days after he moved in, mail started to arrive at that house. It was addressed to a name I did not recognize. He leaves early in the morning for work – or whatever it is he does during the day – so it was easy to sneak a peek at his mail after it was delivered. The name on the mail raised some red flags: Walter Steven Johnson. So typical, so traditional, so *normal*...it has to be fake. I googled him and found a bunch of people with the same name, but none in this city. Tried Facebook, but nada. BIG red flag there. *Everyone* is on Facebook...unless they are trying to hide something. That's just the way it is. So either it's a totally fake name or he really does have some seriously dark secrets. Maybe he's an alien or a clone...or a time-traveling AI from the future. Whoa! I just blew my own mind.

Whatever it is, I will find out. He could be a sex offender, a pedophile. If so, it would be my responsibility to warn the community. It is my duty to find out more. What I'll have to do, I think, is start some real surveillance. I'll keep track of my research in this journal. It could get very interesting!

November 6 Yup, it gets weirder! Walter, or whatever his name is, got home last night just after 6 PM. I was online just doing a little gaming when I heard him pull up in that old pickup truck of his. It's hard to miss – that thing makes a racket. It's annoying, especially when you're enjoying a doobie and trying to have a good time. It broke my concentration, so I logged off and went to the window to watch. I figured any information I could obtain would be helpful. No detail is too small when you're trying to get to the truth. So anyway, I'm watching him get out of his truck and I notice that he's smiling – not just a subtle little smirk, but a big shit-eating, ear-to-ear grin. It was so *suspicious*! What the heck could he be so happy about? What could *anyone* be so happy about? Even stranger, I could have sworn that he was actually *singing* to himself! It was like he didn't even care if anyone could see or hear him. He got out of his truck and went into the house just smiling and singing away. It was ridiculous and embarrassing to watch. No normal person is that happy. Creepy dude!

Anyway, I gamed for a few more hours just killing time and I heard him leave the house again. It was dark by then – had to be close to 9 PM. What could he possibly be doing? Of course, I had to find out. Nefarious activity is best done at night, right? I went to the window and what did I see? He's out there in shorts and a T-shirt, stretching in his driveway! I stood there watching him in disbelief. Guess what he does then? He starts running down the street pumping his arms and legs like a damn fool, as if he's training for a frickin' marathon or something. He went right by my house like that and I swear, he was *still* smiling! The running thing must be a cover, or he really is <u>not</u> right in the head. Now it's crucial that I find out more. Updates soon!

<u>November 7</u> It's 5:30 AM. I went to bed last night thinking about the creepy neighbor and couldn't sleep. Tossed and turned for what felt like hours. I finally did crash sometime after 2 AM and was out for a few hours, but I woke up suddenly as the sun was coming up. I laid there for a while, restless, still thinking about the potential danger of the weirdo next door. I decided to just get out of bed and check on things.

I went to the window and looked out once again at his house. It's now starting to seem extremely spooky. Who knows what kind of bizarre crap goes on behind those closed doors! I saw that he had the lights on, but the shades were drawn. Couldn't see inside, but I knew he was up, probably in the middle of some sick, satanic ritual. I also have a good view of his backyard and, as I'm looking down, the backdoor opened. He came out, illuminated by the light from inside, as it was still dark. I asked myself, *what the heck are you up to?* I didn't want him to see me watching, so I kept the lights in my room off and my head down where he couldn't see me.

My heart started racing as I watched him shut the door and walk into his backyard. I was actually a little scared of what I might witness. I saw him creeping through the shadows as he made his way to a secluded corner of the yard. I made sure to keep my cell phone close in case I needed to call the police...or an exorcist, haha. The thing is, I think somehow he must have known I was watching, because all he did was sit in a lawn chair, fold his hands in his lap, and stay there like that, motionless and apparently silent, for over 20 minutes. What was *that* all about? It looked like he was praying or meditating, but I seriously doubt that. No one really has time for that stuff, or does it in private, especially not this guy. He's weird, but not *that* weird. No, I think he probably knew I was watching. I bet I caught him preparing to do something really freaky. It just keeps getting creepier! Time to take my investigation to the next level.

November 7 It's evening now. The neighbor is not human. I'm convinced of that. I spent the day doing more research online and was only able to find a few tiny bits of information on Mr. Walter Steven Johnson. He was born, apparently, but at this point even *that* is questionable. He could very well be a demonic spirit inhabiting a bio-robot. I also found out he grew up and went to school in another city. He does have a valid driver's license. I could not, however, find anything remotely personal, like what he does for a living, if he is or has ever been married, or has kids or a criminal record. Nothing. Could not even find cell phone records, which is truly astonishing. Do you know *anyone* who doesn't have a cell phone? Isn't that suspicious?

He doesn't appear to use Facebook, Twitter, Instagram, Google Plus or anything else that normal people use. For all I know he doesn't even have an internet connection! That would be utterly shocking, almost inconceivable.

November 8 My online research is going nowhere, so I had to resort to a more hands-on approach. Today was garbage collection day on our street, so I waited for him to leave for work this morning and then went over to have a peek in his bins. What I saw disturbed me and convinced me that my suspicions were well-founded. Get this: there was barely *anything* in the garbage bin! He's been in that house for more than a week and that bin was nearly empty. I dug through it a little and from what I could tell, he doesn't eat much of anything except fruit, fish, bread, and peanut butter. Are you kidding me? There is no way a grown man can live on such insubstantial food. No way he could keep himself fed well enough to run like he does...or even stay conscious, for that matter!

Unless, of course, he simply isn't *human*. What if he really is an alien? Or a traveler from another dimension where lifeforms don't need as many calories as we do? This whole situation is getting a little too paranormal for my taste.

The only way to get to the bottom of this enigma is to find a way into that house...without his knowledge, of course. If he finds out I'm on to him it could put me, and maybe the entire community, in grave danger. He might possess some seriously powerful psychic mojo. If so, I'm probably already screwed, so I may as well keep seeking the truth. Time to plan a covert infiltration mission!

November 9 So here's the deal: When he leaves for work this morning, I'm going to attempt to enter the house from one of the windows in the back. If I can get in without too much trouble, I'll take a look around and see if I can find anything out of the ordinary. I may also see if it's possible to hide a webcam inside for further surveillance. I know it seems risky (and illegal) but I trust my instincts and I know in my gut that there is something *wrong* with this guy. When I find out exactly what he's hiding, my suspicions and efforts will be validated. The mission commences in minutes. I will be back to write my findings soon.

10 AM Wow, just *wow*. I didn't think this could get

any stranger, but I'm here to tell you now that the insanity has just escalated to a whole new level. After watching him drive away in his truck, I dressed entirely in black and snuck over into his yard. I was real stealthy, like I was playing a video game or something. I wore gloves and brought a backpack filled with stuff I thought I might need – flashlight, gloves, pliers, a screwdriver, etc. I was hoping I wouldn't have to work too hard to get in, but I had tools just in case. I got lucky – he left a window unlocked. All I had to do was lift the thing and I squeezed right in!

It was thrilling – better than a video game! I felt like a secret agent or a Special Forces operative. It was dark in the house. I didn't want to attract any attention by turning on the lights, so I got out the flashlight and used it to look around. Being in that house was like being in *The Twilight Zone!* Such an eerie, surreal place.

The first thing I noticed was how unnaturally *clean* the place seemed. There was no clutter – and hardly any furniture. He had very little food in the kitchen, just healthy crap like pasta and fruit. I think I saw a loaf of bread on the counter. I peeked into the fridge and it was practically empty! I almost expected to see a severed head, an alien fetus, or a brain in a jar, but no – just some milk and more fruits and vegetables.

In the living room, my suspicions were confirmed. No TV and no computer, just a couch, some chairs, and a large shelving unit full of books. I couldn't believe it! This guy truly is a freak. I couldn't help but get excited by my discovery. I wonder if I'm the first to see through the deception.

I had to see the bedroom – I was sure that's where the *really* weird stuff happens. I went upstairs to explore, prepared to find a coffin or a telepod or whatever. Most of the rooms were empty, but there was a small bed in one of them. The bed was unmade. There was a small pile of clothes on the floor. A glass of water and a paperback novel sat on the nightstand. It was all a little too *normal*. I was creeped out.

I had seen enough. It was clear to me that the whole house was set up to look like an average working bachelor lived there, but I could sense something sinister lurking beneath the surface. There were so many details that were wrong – just *wrong*...I was starting to feel very uncomfortable. I had to get out of there before my mind unraveled completely. Before I lost my nerve, I was able to hide a tiny, wireless webcam on his bookshelf. It should allow me to see anything he does in his living room. We are through the looking glass, people! Haha.

It's evening. I have to type fast. This might be my last entry – possibly my last words ever. The neighbor just got home – early! I finished configuring my computer to monitor the webcam I installed. It's working great! I was watching the screen when I saw him turn on the lights in the living room. The picture was really clear. I was impressed. He stood there for a moment in the doorway, then I saw this weird look appear on his face, like he could sense I was watching him. Then, without hesitating for a moment, he went straight to the bookshelf and looked directly into the camera. I saw a huge grin spread across his face. While smiling at the lens – smiling at *me* – he shook his head and wagged a finger. This is going to sound crazy, but his pupils actually started to glow red! I saw pure, ancient evil, in those eyes. I knew I was in very serious trouble. He reached for the camera and, before I lost the signal, I'm almost sure I saw the glint of fangs in his mouth.

I think he's on his way over. In fact, I think I hear him at the door right now knocking! There's no way I'm going to answer. That would be madness! If I don't write anything further beyond this entry, please tell my friends and family that I love them and that I'm sorry. Warn the community!

The Invasion

Thomas was a quintessentially contemporary twenty-something of average build and intellect. He was a dispassionate consumer and an ambivalent observer – a sardonic, self-absorbed young man with little ambition and no real goals.

Thomas was an avid follower of pop culture. He was popular on social media, a tech-savvy, jaded master of the internet, and totally ordinary. He spent his days at a computer in a large call center, high-pressure selling mobile phone plans. He spent his nights at a computer at home, immersed in the richly detailed virtual world of a popular role-playing game.

As fate would have it, this typical individual would soon be caught up in events of the most inexplicable variety. Thomas was about to stumble upon evidence of a large scale, clandestine takeover of the planet by hidden, malevolent entities. He was about to be thrust into the role of potential savior of the human race.

It began on a day like any other. Thomas arrived for work less than fully rested, having stayed up late into the night playing his game. He shuffled into the building feeling distant, a hazy fog clouding his head. As he approached his workstation, he noticed that many of his coworkers had been given cubicle upgrades. It was the company's way of incentivizing the employees and rewarding good behavior and strong performances.

Successful salespeople were allowed to have a few personal trinkets on their desk or a family photo or two on the wall. If one performed really well, a door would be installed. The exceptional employees – the die-hard, ruthless, predatory sellers – would have their entire cubicle hydraulically lifted two feet off the floor, so that they were actually elevated above the others.

Thomas could see, to his chagrin, that his cubicle had received no such upgrades. On the contrary, a wall had been removed and his chair replaced with an unfinished wooden box. It was going to be a rough day.

"Sucks to be you," he heard someone say from behind a pale green cubicle wall. He didn't respond. "That's a bummer, bro," insisted the voice. Thomas peered over the wall. It was Corey, another cog in the marketing machine. "Lost a wall...shitty deal, bro," said Corey, clearly enjoying Thomas' predicament.

Thomas noticed that Corey now had a video game character bobblehead toy perched beside his monitor. The character was an anthropomorphic rabbit from a popular game – its head was seemingly nodding in approval of Corey's less-than-sympathetic commentary.

Thomas sighed. "Well, Corey, worse things have happened." Little did he know, at that moment, how true this statement was.

Corey laughed obnoxiously. "Dude! Try, like, showing up on time...or literally working or something." Corey loved the word 'literally' and he constantly misused it. "No worries, bro," Corey continued. "We'll hook up later for, like, a beer or some shit."

"Sounds good." Thomas had no real intention of following through with such a plan. He could only tolerate Corey in small doses. Thomas took a seat on the wooden box in his cubicle.

Thomas powered on the computer. A login screen appeared on the monitor. He typed his name and password into the empty fields and prepared to do the job for which he was nominally paid for. Normally, at this point, his screen would display a long list of names and numbers – potential customers – his targets for the day. This time, however, the screen remained dark.

Thomas punched some keys at random. Still nothing happened. "Oh, come *on*..." he said quietly...but not quietly enough.

"What's up, bro?" Corey asked from the adjacent cubicle.

"Technical issues. Don't worry about it."

Corey grunted and resumed dialing. Within moments, Thomas could hear him mindlessly, mechanically launching into the sales pitch: "Good morning, sir. I'm calling on behalf of..." Thomas tuned it out. Just hearing those first few words made him grimace and shiver with revulsion. *I hate this job*, he thought. *I hate this job with a passion.*

Thomas sat for a short spell, contemplating the unresponsive computer and, in another chamber of his mind, the state and direction of his young life. He considered summoning a supervisor. He considered walking off the job. Instead, he apathetically tapped a few more random keys. Still no response. "Ugh!" he cried, and punched an angry fist into the keyboard...suddenly the screen came to life – a bright, white background with three words in large, bold type dead-center:

WE ARE HERE.

The screen flashed in a strobe-like manner for a few seconds and then went black. Thomas sat motionless, stunned. *What was that?* Those three simple, little words – so innocuous, yet somehow imbued with a dreadful, threatening menace – had he really seen that? Was it a glitch? A prank, perhaps? He could still hear Corey mindlessly reciting the sales script to some poor sucker on the other end of the line. *Overtired*, he thought. *Overactive imagination. Too many video games and movies...too many obscure, esoteric websites. Get a grip!*

Thomas hesitatingly lowered an extended, trembling index finger to the keyboard. He gently poked an arbitrary key. Nothing happened. He exhaled, mostly relieved, but slightly, oddly, disappointed. "Hey, Corey...you on a call? I've got a question for – " The screen burst to life again and once more, a bright, white background with three simple words dead center in large, bold type appeared:

IT'S TOO LATE.

Thomas felt adrenaline flood his chest. There was a throbbing sensation in his temple now, like insects trying to escape his skull...or burrow into his brain. "What in the..." he muttered. "This has to be a joke." Immediately, two words appeared on the monitor:

NO JOKE.

Intuition told Thomas that the situation was indeed no joke – something sinister and very serious was happening. Thomas felt a sudden desire to leave his cubicle and get as far away from the computer as possible. As if reading his mind, the monitor instantaneously displayed four new words:

THERE IS NO ESCAPE.

"Okay, okay...I'm done here," Thomas said. He reached down and pushed a button, shutting down the computer. Part of him expected it to autonomously power up again in defiance, but it remained dormant. Relieved, he stood up, ready to flee this awful place. He wasn't able to avoid the attention of Corey. "Going somewhere, bro?"

"I'm really not feeling well. Going home," Thomas replied.

"Not gonna look good, buddy! Could cost you another wall."

"Don't care."

Thomas walked away before Corey could respond.

He considered talking with a supervisor and asking to be excused for the day due to illness, but it occurred to him that he could simply walk away and never return. The idea greatly pleased him. The impulse was too strong to ignore. Thomas gathered his belongings, left the cubicle, and walked straight out of the building, never once looking back. It felt wonderful. Now he was going home to rest and to put the day's upsetting events behind him.

Once at home, Thomas could finally relax. He was not overly concerned with his current state of unemployment. He was bright enough and had sufficient experience to find a similar job with relative ease. Now, though, he had the rest of the day to enjoy himself. There was no doubt about how he would do that.

Thomas retrieved his laptop computer and sat down in his favorite recliner. He powered the machine on and booted up his favorite game. Thomas was excited that he could now spend the rest of the day - and night, if he wanted – playing his game. He was eager to level up a new character he had created.

The game finished loading. Thomas felt like a kid again, giddy with anticipation, enthusiastic about playing with his toys. *Good times*, he thought. *Yeah.* Thomas began to move his character, a lumbering, cartoonish ogre wielding a giant ax, through the virtual environment. His brain waves were just beginning to slip into a lower frequency when he noticed some text appear in the chat box at the bottom of the screen:

WE ARE HERE.

Seriously? Again? Gotta be hackers or internet trolls, Thomas thought. Still, he was alarmed – rattled enough to consider cutting his game session short. "I can't let these guys spook me," he said aloud. "That's exactly what they want."

Instead of exiting the game, Thomas chose to engage 'Them' in conversation.

"You don't scare me," he typed into the chat box. "I know who you are." Both statements were lies. An instant response:

YES, WE DO AND NO, YOU DON'T.

"Ok, who are you?" he typed. "I'll play along. Got nothing better to do. Could be fun!"

WE FEED ON YOU.

That bit was actually quite creepy. Thomas was genuinely unnerved. He reached for an open can of soda. Before his fingers closed around it, new text appeared:

DRINK UP. IT WON'T HELP.

Thomas' sense of unease grew to immense proportions. Anxiety gripped his mind. Paranoid thoughts cascaded through his brain: *Am I being watched? Do I have unseen enemies? Are they tying to destroy me? Am I going crazy?*

He slammed the laptop computer shut, set it down on the floor, and pushed it away as if it had suddenly transformed into some vile creature. He felt disoriented, panicky, violated. He needed to collect his wits and gather his thoughts. *Easy there, big guy,* he told himself. *Don't lose it.* He stood up, went to the kitchen, and splashed cold water on his face. He felt marginally better. *I need to talk to someone. I need to ground myself to reality.* He decided to call a friend.

As always, his mobile phone was in his front pocket, instantly accessible. With a nimble swipe of a finger, it was unlocked and ready for use. He adroitly manipulated the device and was soon browsing his contact list. He just needed to hear a human voice right now...any voice. As he was perusing his extensive list of friends and family, he heard the familiar sound of his phone's notification system. He had just received a new text message. With another quick swipe of his

agile fingers, this message was displayed:
WE ARE HERE. WE FEED ON YOU. THERE IS
NO ESCAPE.
There was no name or number attached to the
message. It was if the phone itself was communicating with
him. Thomas dropped the device. *Gotta get out of here,* he
thought. *This is insane.*

A primal flight response drove him from his
apartment and out into the street. Thomas lived downtown,
and as was typical for a weekday afternoon, there were
people everywhere going about their business. It was a
bustling mass of humanity. To his absolute horror, Thomas
noticed that each of them, every single man, woman, and
child, had a mobile device in their hands. Some were texting,
some talking, others staring blankly at the screens, but they
were all entirely preoccupied with their insidious little
machines.
An epiphany struck Thomas with force. A screen was
lifted from his eyes and, for the first time, he could see the
world with clarity. He had come to the realization that an
invasion had occurred – a covert infiltration by sentient,
malevolent, parasitic entities. Why they had revealed
themselves to Thomas he did not know, but he understood
that they were indeed feeding on human beings. Were they
technological in nature, or did they use technology to attach
themselves to us? He couldn't be sure.
What was clear, though, was that these entities fed on
the energy, the vitality, the lifeforce of their human hosts.
Almost every person in the developed world has a computer,
a tablet, or a cell phone – and technology is spreading – the
parasites are spreading. Thomas wondered if it was too late
to engage others and warn them of the invasion using direct,
face-to-face, verbal communication.

The Freaks

In the year 1993, the world hung, briefly suspended, between ages. On the cusp of the internet era, driving headlong toward the singularity with unstoppable momentum and reckless abandon, the planet was transforming – mankind was transforming, changing in ways that were either evolutionary or regressive, depending on your perspective. The world was on the edge of the dawn of the great, technological utopia, or, in the view of some, about to cross the threshold into a new and fearsome dark age.

In the year 1993, Joey MacKaye was a 16-year old kid living in a small town deep in the dense woods of Northern Ontario, Canada. He had recently moved there from Vancouver, British Columbia – the move had not only carried him nearly all the way across the vast, beautiful, and formidable country, but also transplanted him from the comfort and familiarity of big city life to a small, strange town in the middle of the bush. He left behind the sights and sounds that he had grown accustomed to, the streets he had called his own through childhood, and the friends with whom he had developed deep, true bonds.

Joey and his single mother arrived in the town of Tempest, Ontario in the late summer. Joey's mother had accepted a new job at a local law firm. The career change, and her desire to distance herself from a troubled past, had motivated the monumental move across the country. Their accommodations – a small, rustic home on the lake – were provided by the firm. Joey's mother was extremely excited about the new life that awaited them in Tempest. Joey was not so enthusiastic.

It was late evening when they pulled up to their new

home nestled in the woods. The setting sun over the lake was picturesque. Joey's mother got out of the car first, a broad smile illuminating her face. Joey, despite the beauty of the scene before him and his mother's genuine joy, remained in the passenger seat sulking.

"Isn't this place just *wonderful*, Joey?" His mother was enraptured. "Isn't it *so* much better than the smog and congestion of Vancouver? I love it here already!"

Joey was not so impressed. "It's...nice," he mumbled.

"You're going to learn to love it here," his mother said as she gathered a suitcase and a few bags from the car. They had sold or given away most of their possessions prior to the move in an attempt to make the transition easier and as a way to further distance themselves from the past. Joey resented this, among many other things.

Joey got out of the car and retrieved a gym bag and electric guitar from the backseat – his only belongings, except for a few small boxes of personally significant items that he had kept. He slung the gym bag and guitar over his shoulder and followed his mother up the steps and onto the front porch of the house.

"This house needs a lot of work," Joey said, kicking at a loose board on the porch.

"That *attitude!*" his mother exclaimed as she unlocked the door and stepped into their new home. "Why do you always have to be so negative? You sound just like your father. He could be a real..." She caught herself before finishing the sentence.

"Dad wouldn't have moved us all the way across the damn country to live in some hick town in the middle of nowhere."

"There's aren't enough snooty restaurants and boutiques here for your father and his new wife," Joey's mother said. It was difficult for her to pass up an opportunity to sneak in a jab at her ex-husband.

"Cindy is actually very nice. You don't know her."

Joey's mother winced. "I'm sure she is."

"She makes dad happy, you know."

"That's good, but my concern is for *your* happiness. That's why we're here. I wanted a better life for us...for *you*, Joey."

"Yeah, right," Joey muttered.

They entered the home and with the flick of a switch, Joey's mother filled it with light. The home was fully furnished, and though in need of a little dusting, looked tidy and welcoming. The furniture and décor maintained and enhanced the rustic ambiance. The warm shades of brown and red and the vaulted ceiling with exposed beams made it feel more like a cabin than a house.

"Oh, it's *amazing!*" Joey's mother cried. "It's even better than I imagined. It's a dream come true."

"For *you*," Joey said. "It feels like *Little House on the Prairie* to me. I'm surprised this place even has electricity."

Joey's mother ignored the comments. She was absolutely enthralled with the home.

"So, where's *my* room?" Joey asked with an exaggerated yawn.

"It's a two-bedroom house. You can have your pick."

"Okay, cool." Joey wandered off to explore the home. From the living room, Joey stepped into the kitchen, where a hallway led to the bathroom and bedrooms. Joey went down the hall and directly to the farthest room. He entered and shut the door.

The room was simply and functionally furnished with a bed, a dresser, and a small desk. A window on the north wall provided an unobstructed view of the lake, which lay in grand and peaceful repose at the edge of the property, sparkling in the nascent twilight. Joey recognized the beauty and grandeur, and acknowledged it with a barely audible, "Wow."

Alone in his new room, Joey began to relax. After being trapped in a car with his mother for five long days and 2000 miles, exhaustion, total and debilitating, hit him like a tidal wave. The bed suddenly looked very inviting. He sat down on its edge and bounced a few times. It was good.

Joey retrieved his Sony walkman cassette player from his bag, along with a few of his favorite tapes. He popped in Nirvana's album *Nevermind*, strapped on the earphones, and cranked the volume. He lay back and allowed the music to work its furious magic.

Joey lost himself in the drums, the bass, the manic chainsaw guitars, and most of all, the powerful voice of the lead singer, Kurt Cobain. Kurt's voice was raw, yet controlled – caustic and fluid at the same time. Somehow it perfectly captured and contained the collective angst and sensitivities of an entire generation of teenagers. Within the simply arranged pop punk songs, Joey found strength, freedom, unity, and, despite the vaguely dark and depressing lyrics, transcendent joy. The music was invigorating.

Even with the energy blasting directly into his head, fatigue began tugging at Joey's consciousness sometime into the second side of the cassette tape. He did not fight it, and before long, he was drawn into deep sleep.

Joey slept for 12 hours and awoke in a state of confusion. *Where am I? Who am I?* He struggled to return to the surface of reality, but something held him back, like an invisible phantom tethered to his mind. He had a moment of flailing mental panic before he finally broke through into total awareness.

It was early morning. The sun was rising. He was in his new home somewhere deep in the woods of Northern

Ontario. Golden light was streaming into his room, the sounds and smells of the lake and the dense boreal forest carried to his perception on clear, crisp northern air. Joey experienced a delicious instant of true serenity, a brief taste of glory. *Maybe this won't be so bad after all,* he thought. He lay there and soaked in the moment, lingering near the threshold of sleep.

The tranquility vanished with a shout.

"Joey! Joey, get up! I need your help." It was his mother calling from somewhere down the hall. Her voice had an effect like shards of glass piercing his brain. Joey groaned and got up slowly.

Joey's mother was waiting for him in the kitchen. "I know it's summer, but there are still things that need to get done around here," she said. "You can't sleep your life away."

"I bet I could."

"Help me unpack this stuff, please." Joey's mother was referring to a small collection of boxes on the kitchen counter.

"Ugh," Joey protested. "Do you really need my help for this? There's, like, just some dishes and silverware in these..."

"That *attitude!*" Joey's mother said once again. "Have you ever tried just being happy? I know it's not cool, but you might like it."

"Anything here to eat?" Joey asked, his voice dripping with insolence. "*That* would make me happy."

"I haven't gone for groceries yet. Unpack this stuff and I'll take you out for breakfast."

Joey's mother left the kitchen and Joey began unpacking the boxes. He was surprised when the sight of the dishes they had used in Vancouver made him nostalgic. The items were imbued with memories, infused with past associations and experiences. A wave of unexpected sadness and deep yearning washed over him. He finished the task as quickly as he could.

Joey found his mother in the living room, crouched behind the floor model television set that the home owners had provided.

"Finished unpacking that stuff," Joey said.

"Mmm, okay, honey," his mother responded, preoccupied with wires and cables.

"Gonna go for a walk, I think," Joey said. His mother looked up from behind the television set. "Don't you want some breakfast?" she asked. "We're only a few minutes away from downtown. We can walk together if you want."

"This place has a downtown?" Joey was incredulous. To him it felt like they were totally isolated in the middle of the bush. "Maybe I'll go exploring then. I'd like to see 'downtown' for myself."

"Just keep an open mind," Joey's mother said. "This is a nice, quaint town."

"Hicksville."

"Once you make some friends you're going to fit right in."

"Somehow I doubt that."

His mother was studying him closely. "Just give it a chance," she said. "Can you do that?"

Joey could see the concern on his mother's face. "I'll try, mom," he said. He didn't really want to worry or upset her.

"Do you need any money?" his mother asked.

"I have a few bucks, but thanks."

"Okay. Have fun, honey. Be safe."

"I will," Joey said as he approached the door.

"Joey?" his mother called as he stepped out onto the patio. "Thank you for helping me unpack. I love you, buddy."

"I love you, too, mom."

Joey shut the door and stood on the patio. A sense of the potential adventure awaiting him in this new and unexplored territory lifted his spirits. He felt, for perhaps the first time since they had left British Columbia, real excitement – the anticipation of an unwritten future. *I can be whoever I want to be,* he thought. *No one here knows me. I could completely reinvent myself.* It was an empowering idea.

Joey stepped off the patio and began walking. He felt, for the moment, like a free-range lion, on the prowl in the early morning jungle.

The home that Joey and his mother now occupied was on a quiet street that led into the heart of Tempest. Joey walked the tree-lined sidewalk, taking it all in. *This really is a small town,* he thought. *Nothing at all like the hustle and madness of Vancouver.* As he walked, he gained confidence. As he gained confidence, his stride transformed into a cocky swagger.

I'm a badass, Joey thought. *This town won't know what hit 'em.*

Within a few blocks, the dense forest was replaced by a quiet residential area. The heavy bush blended smoothly into a neighborhood of large, aging war-era houses. Most homes were in need of repair – some were minimally weathered, others were extremely dilapidated. A few homes seemed to be abandoned and condemned. It was clear to Joey that the neighborhood had seen better days. Still, a certain charming small town character remained.

Joey had been walking for about 15 minutes when he arrived at Tempest's main street, which was, of course, called Main Street. A small stretch of storefronts served as downtown Tempest. It was an area of no more than four square blocks. Joey was not surprised. "Somehow, I doubt I'll find a cool record store around here," he said.

There was minimal activity on the street on this late summer morning. The few people Joey encountered carried themselves in a languid, easy manner. The hardware store and the barber shop seemed to be the hottest attractions. Joey walked on, until he found himself in front of a building that actually seemed to have some real *life* – the pool hall on the corner. A gaudy neon sign in the window identified the establishment as Wizard's Billiards. *Nice,* Joey thought. It had a seedy quality that instantly appealed to him.

As he stood peering into the window, the door flew open, and out stepped a couple of characters straight out of an '80s heavy metal video. Two guys in leather, denim, and Metallica t-shirts burst out onto the street and whipped out cigarettes, lighting them with practiced panache. Their mullet hair cuts and peach fuzz mustaches were ten years out of style.

"You suck, dude," the tall one said to the shorter. "You cost us that game. Fuck."

And then they saw Joey standing there – instant tension. The metal heads immediately recognized Joey for what he was – a stranger to town. The hostility they radiated toward him was thick and nasty. They eyed Joey up and down in an exaggerated gesture. Joey wore clothes vaguely in alignment with the current grunge trend, but for the most part he followed no particular style. He took pride in being an individual, and had worn the same ensemble of jeans, t-shirt, and buttoned overshirt since grade seven.

"Hey, buddy," the short one said with a sneer. "What's up?"

The words were innocuous, but the moment was ripe with danger. An imminent threat of violence hung in the air. *A couple of typical meatheads,* Joey thought – but what he said was: "Not much, guys. New to town. Just looking for a place to chill." Though he felt shaky and nervous, he made a valiant attempt to project a calm exterior.

The headbangers were confused. Apparently the local kids were easily intimidated. They were not sure how to handle Joey's unexpected response to their veiled taunts. They looked at each other, perplexed, their mouths open, their eyes dull and questioning. "Huh," the tall one muttered before taking a long drag on his cigarette.

"Do you play?" the short one asked, motioning toward the pool tables inside the hall.

"A little," Joey replied, "but it's been a long time. My dad taught me to play when I was a kid."

"Are you any good?" the tall banger asked, dragging hard on his cigarette until he was inhaling filter.

"Not really," Joey responded honestly.

The short banger scoffed. "Gotta be good to play on these tables," he said.

"Fair enough," Joey said.

"Unless you wanna, you know...make it interesting," the tall one smirked. The heavy metal casualties exchanged looks like predators coordinating an attack. Their intent was obvious to Joey.

"Nah. I'm not really into gambling."

"One game," the short banger insisted. "Just a small wager between buds. All in good fun."

"No thanks, guys. I'm kinda broke."

"What are ya, a *pussy?*" the tall one sneered.

So cliché, so comical, Joey thought. *These guys have seen too many bad teen movies.* His awareness of the tactics employed by the two metal heads did not leave him entirely immune to their taunts. He could feel volatile emotions building within him: embarrassment, vulnerability, a sick anger that was rapidly building to an intense fury. He recognized that he was in danger of escalating the situation if he was not careful.

"Look at the way he dresses," the short banger said. "Maybe he's a fag." The words flew from his mouth like poisoned darts.

"Hey guys, I really don't want any trouble," Joey said, taking a step back. He was beginning to feel flustered and shaky. He hadn't been in a real fistfight since grade school. It was ridiculous and almost unbelievable that he was on the verge of an actual punch-up.

The tall banger produced a small flask from the pocket of his tasseled and studded leather jacket. The jacket appeared to be a few sizes too small for him. The banger unscrewed the cap of the flask, took a deep pull, and passed it to his short companion.

"Well, maybe you should go back to where you came from," the tall banger said.

Joey's fear was eclipsed by indignation. *Can't let these assholes intimidate me,* he thought. He made a childish, irrational decision. Instead of walking away, he fell for their transparent mind game.

"You know, I quite like it here," Joey said. "I think I'll stay. In fact, I think I *am* in the mood for a game after all." Joey moved toward the door to the pool hall. The two metal heads, who had been standing to the side, now closed in, blocking the entrance.

Defiantly, foolishly, Joey made an effort to squeeze past them. The tall metal head did what cartoon buffoons generally do in such situations: he planted his hands on Joey's shoulders and shoved. It was a rather weak push, the negligible force of which simply caused Joey to take a few steps back. The small banger snickered.

"Excuse me, fellas," Joey said. "I do believe you are in my way."

"You're cruisin' for a bruisin'," the tall banger said. "You're about to be in a world of hurt."

"Is my ass grass?" Joey asked.

Before the mockery in Joey's retort could register in the tall banger's pot-and-beer-addled brain, the door to the pool hall opened behind him. A young man stepped out, humming a Broadway show tune and snapping his fingers. Pushing his way through the leather-jacketed duo, the young man stepped into the fray. "Everything cool here, Chad?" he said, addressing the tall banger.

The young man who had suddenly appeared wore a black trench coat with a large collection of pins and buttons adorning its wide lapels. Beneath the coat, a t-shirt with a prominent Dead Kennedy's logo was visible. His hair was black and spiked. Cherry-colored Dr. Martens boots completed the look.

"Nothing you need to worry about, Steve," the tall banger said. They were apparently well acquainted.

"This little prick has a big mouth," the short banger spat.

"Is that so?" inquired Steve. He took a moment to ponder Joey, rubbing his chin quizzically with a finger and thumb. Joey shrugged. Steve sized up the short banger similarly. "Seems to me like your mouth is actually a few millimeters bigger by my estimation, Duane."

Duane's face turned red. He raised a fist to head level and made a twitchy motion as if he were about to punch Steve. It was all bravado, an empty threat – the last resort of an insecure, threatened child on the playground. "Fag," he said.

Chad scoffed. "Fuck these guys." The words were hostile yet devoid of real menace. Though he was actually much taller, there was an unusual dynamic to their interactions that suggested that Chad respected – even feared – Steve.

"Let's go shoot some stick," Chad said. "Give these

butt buddies some privacy."

"Hahaha," chortled Duane. "Butt buddies. Yeah. See ya later, *fags!*"

The two head bangers disappeared back into the pool hall.

"Don't worry about Beavis and Butthead," Steve said. "Those cro-mags are, like most bullies, essentially harmless. Chad used to give me a hard time, until I fought back a few years ago and put him on his ass. Now I just run intellectual cartwheels around him whenever he needs to be put into his place. You know how it is..."

"I knew guys like that back in Van," Joey said.

"You from Vancouver?"

"Yup, just moved here with my mom."

"Why?" Steve seemed truly astonished.

"My mom got a job here. I had no choice. My dad lives with his new wife and isn't really involved any more. Typical story, right?"

"That sucks, dude. I'm sorry. My parents are divorced too. Only interested in themselves. I learned a *long* time ago that you can't really trust anyone – especially adults. I'm Steve, by the way. Welcome to Tempest, Ontario...or as I like to call it, The Mistake by the Lake."

"I'm Joey. This seems like a nice enough town."

"It's a total shithole. I'm getting the hell out of here as soon as I can. Toronto, Montreal, maybe even Vancouver...anywhere but here. I want to be in a city with an actual music scene, you know?"

"Do you play?"

"Not really. I've been working on lyrics, though. Always wanted to start a band, just never met the right people. In this town, you gotta play classic rock or hair metal...cheesy-ass cock rock."

"I got a guitar for my last birthday. Been teaching

myself how to play. I'm still pretty shitty, but I'm getting better. I learned a few Nirvana songs, a couple of Soundgarden riffs, part of a Pearl Jam song..."

"That's cool. Grunge is okay, but I like *good* music."

"Like what?"

"Mostly punk and hardcore. DK, Black Flag, Minor Threat, The Exploited, Crass, The Clash, The Pistols, 7 Seconds...you know, *good* music."

"Cool." Joey had only heard of a few of the bands Steve mentioned. His exposure to new music had been largely limited to radio and the videos he saw on MuchMusic, the self-appointed "Nation's Music Station!"

"We should start a band," Steve said.

The two young men fell into an easy rhythm as they walked up the sidewalk away from the pool hall. They became instant friends, implicit in the way they developed a quick, comfortable rapport. Through shared experience, mutual recognition of similar values, and mysterious forces at work behind the scenes, Joey and Steve bonded. As is the case in all fate-assigned relationships, it was as if they had known each other their entire lives.

The last days of summer ebbed away and autumn arrived as it does in Northern Ontario – blustery, chilly, and way too soon. Seemingly overnight, the region was transformed from a lush forest of deep greens to a fall wonderland of warm shades of red, yellow, and orange. The low temperatures and changing colors signaled an end to the summer heat and, for the young people of the town of Tempest, the end of carefree days of no school and little responsibility.

Joey started attending classes at the only public high school in town – Tempest Collegiate Institute, or TCI, as most residents referred to it. Joey's mother started her new job at a local law firm. Their small family began the process of assimilating into their new environment. For Joey, the process was difficult.

Most of the kids at TCI had known Steve since early childhood. They had grown up together, their parents knew each other, and, regardless of Steve's iconoclastic, rebellious, sardonic nature, they accepted him. He was a weirdo, but he was local.

Joey was not so lucky. He got along well with Steve, but he was finding it difficult to fit in. Joey had not established a place in the social hierarchy of the small town kids. He did not dress as they did. He did not share the same hobbies. He was not into snowmobiling, hunting, drinking, and hockey. He was different and they recognized it. It was not long before he became a target.

It started in a relatively benign fashion – bad vibes, dirty looks, whispered insults. The popular kids were fiercely protective of the established order. The new kid from the big city with the sharp intellect and creative streak was a threat. Joey's precarious social position became clear one typical Monday morning during the second week of the school year.

Joey was making his way from a room on the 2nd floor, where he had just endured an excruciating 45 minutes of Canadian history delivered in dreadful monotone, to the school's basement. He was enthusiastically anticipating his favorite class of the day – visual arts. Although he was finding it difficult to truly fit in, he was becoming more comfortable at the school. His exposure to the small town discriminatory attitude strengthened his sense of individuality. Joey sort of liked being the new guy. It made him feel unique. He walked the halls now with an attitude. He was about to be tested.

In the stairwell between floors, he was confronted by

TCI's male power duo, Bradley and Shane. Bradley was a doctor's son with the arrogance and malevolence that takes a lifetime of privilege to cultivate. He wore name brand sweaters and jeans. He kept his slick blond hair meticulously cut in the style of the era's popular boy bands. He was, in Steve's definition, a total Preppie...and a complete tool. Shane was Bradley's ever-present sidekick, his lackey and minion. At six foot four and over 250 pounds, he was the star of the football team and was widely considered the toughest guy at the school. He was a prototypical, classic jock. Bradley and Shane were popular and feared – adored by most and reviled by a silent few.

Joey was alone when Bradley and Shane cornered him. It was not the first time they had encountered each other. Having known similar types back in Vancouver, Joey's instinct had been to avoid conflict by giving the duo a wide berth when their paths happened to cross. This time, however, the pair of high school superstars took the opportunity to flex their social muscles with a metaphorical territorial pissing.

As Joey made an attempt to pass by on the landing, Shane stepped into his path, blocking his way. He simply stood there silently, glaring down at Joey with his chest puffed out behind his Toronto Argonauts half-shirt. Joey sighed.

"Where you goin', *freak?*" Shane spit the words out like toxic rain.

"Class," Joey said. The volatility of the moment was apparent. He knew he would have to play it carefully. He attempted to slide past Shane and continue down the stairs. Bradley stepped in beside Shane, forming an impenetrable line.

"*Class,*" Bradley mocked in a silly, feminine voice.

"Freak," Shane repeated. It was an overly-used

regional insult, applied to anyone who deviated even slightly from the norm.

"Unfortunately, it's true," Joey said. "As much as I'd love to stay and chat with you two fine gentleman, there is a class I must attend. So, if you'll excuse me..."

Bradley jumped back with his hands up in an exaggerated display of deference. "Oh, dear *me!*" he said. "Are we in your way? So *sorry!*"

"No problem," Joey said, playing along. He again tried to squeeze through, but was thwarted by a sidestepping Shane, who moved as if he were making a play on the field.

"Is there a problem, guys?" Joey asked. Adrenaline flowed. Taut and twitchy, Joey's muscles vibrated with anxious energy. Fluid fear coursed through his veins. Fight or flight instinct heightened his awareness. Sensory impressions increased in intensity. His brained throbbed, in his mind a siren blared: *Threat! Threat! Threat!*

"Yeah, there's a problem," Bradley sneered.

Shane poked Joey in the chest with a beefy finger. "*You're* the problem, freak," he said.

Joey found himself repeating the words he had used in his encounter with the metal heads at the pool hall: "Hey guys, I really don't want any trouble."

"Who the fuck do you think you are?" Bradley asked. "We *own* this school."

"You should go back to Edmonton," Shane said.

Vancouver, idiot, Joey thought. He considered correcting him, but wisely chose not to.

"What makes you think you can walk around here like a fuckin' tough guy?" Bradley asked. "Are you under the impression that you *belong* here or something? Because, if so, you are greatly mistaken."

Joey kept quiet. It was clear that anything he said would only further incite his teenage tormentors. He steeled himself and remained stoic.

"What's the matter?" Shane taunted. "Ain't ya got anything to say?"

"I think he shit himself," Bradley said, leaning in and taking a sniff. "Sure smells like it. You fuckin' *stink*, dude. Did you know that?" Joey maintained eye contact, his expression blank.

Just as the severity of the situation escalated and the threat of violence grew, the sound of fast-approaching footsteps from above disrupted the scene. The rapid footsteps of the individual descending the stairs was accompanied by loud and frantic singing – or, more precisely, screaming.

"I fought the law and I won, I fought the law and I won!" Joey immediately recognized the person shouting as Steve. Steve took the final three steps in a joyful bound, landing directly between the Shane-Bradley line and Joey.

"What's up, turd burglars?" Steve said, addressing no one in particular.

"Just having a little chat with the new guy," Bradley said. "None of your business, Steve."

"Everything's cool," Joey said. "We were just taking about the CFL. I think the expansion into the US is a travesty. Shane, I think, would agree."

"Whatever, freak," Shane muttered.

"Go Maple Leafs!" Steve bellowed, miming a baseball bat swing.

"Fuck off," Bradley said.

"Okay, then!" Steve remained cheerful. "Planning on attending art today, Joey? I think it's Kirlian photography day. Don't wanna be late!"

"Yeah, we better get going," Joey said.

As the small gathering dispersed, Bradley glared at Joey. "You better watch yourself, New Guy," he said. "You're going to get hurt if you aren't careful."

"Freak!" Shane shouted.

Joey and Steve continued on their way to the art room, arriving just as class was about to begin. Pausing at the door to the room, Steve addressed Joey in a refreshingly sincere fashion. "I get the sense that you're having a hard time with some of the locals here in our fair city," he said.

"It's been tough," Joey concurred.

"Stay strong, man. Be true to yourself. It's a small town, but the people here are, for the most part, good. They simply have a hard time understanding anyone who is...different. Trust me, I *know*." Steve gave Joey a brotherly slap on the back as they entered the classroom.

The rest of the day passed without further incident. Joey, however, was finding it harder and harder to maintain concentration in his classes. Beneath the surface, anxiety and agitation were beginning to percolate in his already turbulent teenage heart. A maelstrom was brewing in the town of Tempest.

Joey walked home from school alone that afternoon. He arrived to find the house empty, as usual. Joey's mother worked long hours. In the month since they had moved to Tempest, the time they spent together had greatly dwindled. They rarely shared meals. Joey's mother was simply too exhausted in the evening to cook. She often fell asleep in front of the television with a half-eaten frozen dinner in her lap. Joey learned to fend for himself.

On this particular afternoon, Joey needed his mother. He sat at the kitchen table from the moment he got home until she walked through the door many hours later. During the wait, his thoughts raced and his emotions cycled. By the time she stepped into the kitchen and saw him sitting there, Joey was deeply upset. As soon as he saw his mother he began to cry and shake.

"Joey!" his mother exclaimed. "What's wrong?" Shocked, she ran to his side, dropped to her knees, and embraced him as he sat weeping.

"I hate it here, mom," Joey said between sobs. "I want to go home. I want to see dad." The sensation of his mother's embrace caused him to cry harder. He wept now with frightening intensity. The dam had burst.

"Oh, Joey. It's okay, buddy. Things will get easier, I promise."

"You don't know that!" Joey cried. "You don't even know what I've been going through. All you care about is *work.*" He imbued the last word with a generous dose of contempt.

Joey's mother took a seat at the table beside him and clasped his hands in her own, her expression and demeanor compassionate, yet serious. "I need you to be strong, Joey," she said. "I'm doing the best I can."

"I just don't fit in here," Joey said, his composure returning.

"Give it time. You're a great kid. People will see that. It won't be long before you make friends. You're funny, smart, kind...you'll probably end up super popular! You might even meet a girl!" She winked at him.

"Oh, *please,*" Joey said, but he couldn't hide the smirk that appeared on his face. "I don't care about popularity. I really don't. I just want to be able to walk down the street, or down the hall at school, and not have to worry about being insulted...or assaulted."

"Has that happened? Are people bullying you? Have you been fighting?"

Joey processed the question. In their often-strained relationship, Joey and his mother had at least established a level of trust that allowed for honest communication. It was difficult for him to lie to her.

"No," Joey said, "not actual fistfights, just a lot of macho idiots trying to throw their weight around, I guess. Nothing I can't handle, it's just...tedious."

"Have you tried talking to them? I'm sure if they get to know you..."

Joey laughed. "Somehow I doubt that would help."

"That *attitude!* It's no surprise you're having a hard time making friends. Have you been acting like a smartass? People don't like a smartass."

"Just being myself, mom. Sometimes that's all it takes. These people just don't like *me*. Instant hate. It's like I'm an alien or something. Bunch of hicks, anyway..."

"That's not fair and you know it. Treat others the way you want to be treated. That includes keeping an open mind and not judging."

"Hmm..." Joey was thoughtful. He could not deny the truth of his mother's words. Though sometimes disappointed in the choices she made, he admired his mother's wisdom and intelligence.

"I'm doing the best I can to make a better life for us," Joey's mother continued. "Can you work with me? Or at least not make this any harder than it is? We're both adjusting. I just need you to make an effort...and know that I love you." Her eyes had become red and watery. She was getting emotional. Joey could sense that she was on the verge of tears.

"I love you too, mom," Joey said, putting an arm around her shoulders. "I guess I can give it some more time. I'm sure things will work out. I'm just a little weird for this town, but eventually they'll get used to me." Now it was he who winked at her. He did not like to see his mother upset. In that moment, he made a decision to keep his internal struggles private.

After dinner, Joey spent the rest of the evening alone

in his room strumming his battered, second-hand guitar. He only knew a few chords and could barely keep the thing in tune, but playing had become his favorite way to spend time, especially when he was feeling troubled. It was an effective way to release tension. The sensation of the strings beneath his fingers was incredibly satisfying. The unrefined, rugged sound coming from his tiny amplifier perfectly expressed his internal struggles. He had found a way to sublimate his emotions. Music made him feel in control again.

On his way to school the next morning, Joey experimented with optimism. He allowed his imagination to explore various positive scenarios for his near future, including one in which he settled into his new environment, existed in harmony with his peers, and perhaps even found happiness. It was a clear, crisp autumn morning, perfectly suited for daydreaming.

He arrived at school energized, ready for the academic and social challenges ahead. Before he had even stepped through the front door, his resolve was tested. Lost in thought, he did not see Chad and Duane, the headbangers from the pool hall, loitering near the entrance and puffing away on cigarettes.

"Well, looky here," Chad said. "It's the new fag in town."

"What's up, knob gobbler?" Duane grinned like an imbecile.

And so it begins, Joey thought. He ignored the insults and entered the building.

The school was alive with the typical morning commotion and chatter. Students were congregating in the lobby, before fragmenting into small clusters. Cliques and allegiances, friends and enemies, the popular and the outcast, the natural high school order was establishing itself. The hidden engine of the order – the unseen architecture – involved a mysterious, complicated algorithm of socioeconomic and psychological factors.

From Joey's outsider perspective, the social structure seemed random, arbitrary. His young mind could not discern the subtle influences. He stood in the lobby and observed the apparent chaos for a few moments before gathering the strength to enter the melee.

First period for Joey was Advanced English. He merged with the students crowding the narrow halls. He began to make his way toward his assigned locker to pick up the materials he would need for class. Squeezing past a giggling trio of girls with tight sweaters, puffed-up hair, and too much makeup, he found his locker and grasped the combination lock. As he was working the mechanism, he could hear the girls whispering behind his back. He glanced over his shoulder and, sure enough, they were staring right at him, heads together, hands over their mouths, vicious glimmers of pure malevolence sparkling in their heavily mascaraed eyes.

Joey was struck by a wave of self-conscious anxiety. Embarrassment of the highly potent variety that only judgmental teenage girls could administer washed over him. He tried to remain indifferent. He tried to hold on to the indomitable spirit he had mustered on his walk to school. He managed to get his belongings out of the locker before cracking. Ignoring the fiendish snickering, he replaced the lock and continued down the hall.

Now it seemed like everyone in the congested hallway was talking about him. Joey could feel a thousand pairs of eyes burning holes in the back of his head like an array of lasers. He kept his head up and focused on his destination. He made it exactly ten steps from his locker.

From out of a gathering of young men with tidy haircuts, pastel name-brand t-shirts, and acid-washed jeans, a foot suddenly jutted out, catching Joey in mid-stride. He could not catch himself before falling in an awkward, messy heap on the floor. His books went flying. He struck his face on the floor. Blood gushed from his nose. Laughter echoed up and down the hall.

"Hope you had a good trip!" someone yelled.

"See ya next fall!" said another.

"Freak!" shrieked a third.

Joey stood up and gathered his stuff, stopping the flow of blood from his nose with pinched fingers. As he reached for a text book that had landed near the preppy perpetrators, one of them kicked at it, sending it sliding further down the hall. Joey sighed as it traveled away from his reach.

"Very nice," he said. "Well done, guys." Joey summoned his courage, gathered his dignity, and retrieved the wayward book. He continued on his way to class.

It occurred to him how strange it was to be the target of bullying. He was, all things considered, a fairly normal kid. In Vancouver, he had even been nominally popular. He was not exactly a social butterfly, but he had always maintained a small, close circle of friends. Over the last few years, he had even had a few girlfriends. In his estimation, he did not fit the stereotypical victim profile.

Joey's thoughts wandered. He remembered Ricky Talbot, who, in sixth grade, was the recipient of brutal, merciless, verbal and physical abuse by the other students. Joey recalled how, although he never directly participated in the bullying, he had never done anything to stop it. He had never spoken up for Ricky. By tacitly accepting the abuse, he was, in fact, complicit.

Ricky, I feel your pain, he thought. Ricky had been an

awkward, geeky kid with braces, thick glasses, and a speech impediment. Ricky, though obviously hurt by the torment, had come to accept his place in the social hierarchy. Joey, however, was indignant, and determined to rise above the position he was being forced into.

The classroom door was open as Joey approached. He hesitated before entering. *Into the lion's den,* he thought, and plunged through the door.

The other students were already at their desks. The teacher was at the blackboard. Joey found a seat near the back of the room. No one seemed to pay him any attention, but his sense of unease was growing. He squirmed in his seat throughout the lesson, unable to remain focused on what the teacher was saying. The clock, which he glanced at every few seconds, mocked him and his plight. He fantasized about escaping. He wanted nothing more than to be at home playing his guitar.

The class ended. Joey hadn't learned a thing. He drifted out of the room in a daze. He had 15 minutes until his next class. Surrounded once again by the writhing mass of students, swallowed up by the horde, he felt more distant and alone than ever. In their midst, he had the strange sensation that he was somehow existing in another realm, a parallel universe, an alternate dimension that co-existed and shared boundaries with the one the people around him inhabited. He could see and hear them, but they were out of sync and unreachable.

Instead of continuing on to his next class, Joey reflexively stepped out the next available exit. He found himself in a narrow alcove at the side of the school. A small gathering of students were huddled together sharing a cigarette – a circle of misfits and assorted weirdos. Joey was not surprised to see Steve among them. Acrid, blue smoke curled around their heads as they chatted excitedly.

"Joey!" Steve bellowed. "Join us!"

Joey approached the group. Out of the three kids gathered, Joey only recognized Steve. The other two eyed him with curiosity, but accepted him into the circle.

"We were just discussing the *Evil Dead* movies. Have you seen the new one, *Army of Darkness*? Rick here thinks it's shit. I think it's the best of the series. What are your thoughts?"

"Haven't seen it," Joey replied. "*Evil Dead 2* was cool, though." Joey had gone through a horror movie phase a few years back. During the seventh and eighth grades, they were an obsession.

"*Evil Dead 2* rocks," Rick said. "When dude whacks his zombie girlfriend's head off with a shovel...that shit was *awesome!*" Rick was a tall, thin, skateboarder with long, blonde hair. His wore a black sweatshirt beneath a white t-shirt emblazoned with the Thrasher logo. His jeans were ridiculously baggy. He reeked of marijuana. "Too much humor in *Army of Darkness*," he said, "too little gore."

"Point taken," Steve nodded as he took the smoldering, nearly finished cigarette from a small, quiet girl with black hair, black eyeliner, black lipstick, and a grim demeanor standing to his right.

"So, Joey," Steve said, "how has your day been so far at this fine institute of learning?"

"The institution of my discontent," the goth girl mumbled. Her clothing too was entirely black, except for the Siouxsie and the Banshees image on her long-sleeve shirt.

"It started off well," Joey said, "but went quickly downhill when I was knocked on my ass and humiliated in the hall." Steve offered him the last of the cigarette. Joey declined with a subtle but firm gesture. Steve crushed the butt beneath the steel toe of his Doc Martens.

"This school is a cesspool," the goth girl said.

"It isn't a school, Clara, it's a prison," Steve said, "an indoctrination camp, a brainwashing facility."

"Damn right," Rick agreed.

"In the words of the immortal Henry Rollins of the mighty Black Flag on their seminal and massively influential 1981 album *Damaged*: *'Rise above! I'm gonna rise above!'*" Steve shouted the lyrics to a song that clearly had great meaning for him.

"Fuck, yeah," Rick said.

"What this hellhole really needs is a cleansing," Clara said. "Wouldn't it be great to bring a machine gun to school one day and just, you know, mow down all the douchebags, assholes, preps, and jocks?" Clara pantomimed firing an automatic rifle with a huge grin on her pale face. She reveled in her imaginary revenge scenario.

"Yikes," Steve grimaced, "I prefer a more subtle and sophisticated approach. I like your enthusiasm, though! Nice!"

A bell sounded, signaling the start of the next class in five minutes. "Back into the grinder," Steve said. "I'll catch up with you crazy kids later. See ya!" Steve bounded through the door with dramatic flair and disappeared into the school.

"Is he actually going to class?" Rick was incredulous.

"He skipped a few last week," Clara said. "He'll get suspended if he misses any more so soon after. His stepfather would kick his ass if he got suspended."

"Stepfather?" Joey inquired. He had not been aware of Steve's domestic situation.

"Yeah, his parents divorced when he was real young," Clara said. "His mother remarried recently. The new guy is a real asshole. Heavy drinker, abusive, you know the type. He hates Steve and gives him shit constantly."

"I didn't know," Joey said.

"He doesn't like to talk about it," Clara said.

"Dude's got it rough," Rick nodded. "That's why he tries to avoid being at home and is usually chillin' at the arcade or at the park. Remember how he was *before* his mom remarried? He dressed all preppy and shit. He used to hang out with the jocks and bimbos."

"Really?" Joey was truly surprised. He had a hard time visualizing Steve dressed like one of the drones.

"It's true," Clara confirmed. "He changed a lot over the last few years. We dated for a bit, and he opened up to me a few times."

"I remember when you guys were a couple!" Rick blurted. "King and queen of the freaks." Rick chuckled at his own joke.

"Yeah, well, he's a complicated guy," Clara said. "He's got a good heart, though. We're still friends. Anyway, I gotta get to class. Later."

"Later, skater!" Rick cheerfully replied. "I better motor too. See ya."

"Bye," Joey said.

Rick and Clara entered the school. Joey stood alone in the alcove for a few minutes, thoughtful and, considering the altercation in the hallway earlier that morning, oddly serene. He had felt comfortable in the presence of Steve, Rick, and Clara. He got the sense that they understood and accepted him. *Have I actually made friends in this weird little town?* he asked himself. It was an exciting and promising development.

On the way to his next class, a moment of synchronicity occurred. Joey was running late. The halls were empty. A sign on the wall caught his eye, as if placed there specifically for him to see at that precise time. In bold letters, the sign read:

TCI TALENT SHOW
Show your stuff on the stage!
October 15, 1993!
Apply now!

A perfect, simple, wonderful idea coalesced in Joey's mind: *I'm going to start a band and play at that show.* His newly discovered passion for the guitar had been a real source of relief during the difficult transitions he had recently experienced. He found refuge in music. Pursuing his creative impulses allowed him to channel the frustration and pain he had felt into something productive. It gave him control over his emotional state. He visualized himself playing guitar in front of the entire student populace, powerful waves of sound pulsing from his amplifier and washing over the crowd, immersing them in his music. In his mind's eye it was glorious.

Joey thought of Steve, who had mentioned in their first meeting that he had always wanted to start a band. He thought of Rick and Clara. *Wouldn't it be great to play music with other people, on an actual stage?* Joey thought. The idea didn't seem so far-fetched...in fact, it seemed like destiny.

Joey attended the rest of his classes that day and hurried home afterwards. As he expected, the house was empty when he arrived. He rushed directly to his room upon stepping inside. He picked up his guitar and began strumming with fresh vigor and inspiration. He was improving, and he knew it. His fingers found their place on the neck more quickly and intuitively now. His pick hand was much more accurate. His stamina had increased. It was exhilarating.

By the time Joey's mother got home from work, he had worked out a small batch of riffs and rhythms, which he collected by recording them on his portable tape deck. They were short, rough song ideas – ragged little bits of audio – but they were *his* ideas. He was ecstatic and couldn't wait to share his excitement. He ran out of the room with the tape deck the moment he heard the front door open.

Joey's mother looked exhausted. She stumbled through the door like a defeated prize fighter and threw herself on the couch. "What an awful day," she sighed. "Hi, Joey."

"Hi, mom. Do you have a minute? I have something to share..."

"Oh, honey, it's not a good time. Can it wait? I'm really tired."

"Yeah, I suppose so. I'm sorry you had a bad day."

"It could be worse," Joey's mother philosophized. "At least I have a job." She picked up the TV remote from the coffee table and turned on the set. Joey watched as her body relaxed and her mind slipped into a hypnotic state. It made him feel sad for her.

"You're working too hard," Joey said.

"I know, buddy, but somebody's got to pay the bills."

"Can I get you something to eat?"

"I'm okay for now. You eat. I'll get something later."

Joey wandered into the kitchen to find some food. As he was opening a can of soup, he heard his mother snoring in the living room. He looked in and saw her already asleep in the glow of the television set. The insufferable characters from the show *Seinfeld* were babbling away on the screen. Joey took his soup to his room and ate it.

That night, Joey had an extremely difficult time sleeping. His thoughts raced. His head was full of sounds and images. The excitement he felt imagining himself playing in a band was matched by the thrill of discovering a way to transcend his environment. It was not fame nor riches that he desired, but self-discovery and empowerment – control over his own fate and emancipation from his seemingly inexorable fate as a poor, working class slave. The future again seemed full of potential.

Joey did eventually fall asleep and, in the morning, he actually looked forward to going to school. He gathered his things, including the recording he had made of his song ideas, and bolted out the door.

He arrived at school and went to the smoking alcove where, sure enough, Steve and the others had gathered for a puff before class. Joey entered their midst and declared, "We are going to start a band. We are going to play at the talent show. It's going to be awesome."

Steve, Rick, and Clara stared at Joey in disbelief.

"Dude, what have *you* been smoking?" Rick said. "Can I have some?"

"The talent show is a joke," Clara scoffed. "There's no way in hell I'd be a performing monkey for those mindless meatbags."

"I like it," Steve smiled. "When do we start?"

"As soon as possible," Joey replied. "I already have some song ideas." He opened his backpack and retrieved the cassette tape. "Just some riffs, really. They need lyrics." He handed the tape to Steve.

"Excellent," Steve said, admiring the cassette. "You've got some fire in your belly. I'm impressed."

"At the very least, it could be fun," Joey said. "What have we got to lose?"

"Fuck, yeah," Rick said. "Can I be the drummer? My older bro has a kit. He lets me play it sometimes. We could probably even jam at my place!" Rick played air drums like a spastic animal.

"There's nothing else to do around here." Clara was clearly warming up to the idea. "Maybe it's not such a stupid idea after all."

"That's the spirit!" Steve exclaimed.

A group was born, formed from the essence of teenage angst and imagination, forged in friendship.

That very weekend, the four friends gathered in Rick's garage for their first rehearsal. It was a chilly autumn afternoon. They huddled around a space heater that Rick's father had thoughtfully provided. It was the first time any of them had played music in a group setting. Clara had only been playing the borrowed bass that she brought to the rehearsal for a few days. Steve had never sung in public. Rick and Joey had the most experience, but it was minimal at best. The group stood there awkwardly, unsure of how to proceed.

"I've been listening to your riffs," Steve finally said to Joey. "I came up with some lyrics."

"That's awesome!" Joey beamed.

"Shouldn't we tune up or something?" Clara said. She strapped on her bass and plugged it into a small amp.

"Ya, I guess so," Joey said, slinging the strap of the guitar over his shoulder. He too plugged in and began plucking away at the strings one by one, starting with the low E. Clara attempted to match the pitch of her strings to his. While they were still attempting to tune their instruments, Rick started banging away on the drums. It was a cacophonous mess.

Steve stepped in to provide some order. "As much as I like noise rock, I think we should get organized and try to work on, you know, actual *songs*," he said.

It took a few minutes of sonic stumbling, but eventually the guitars were in tune, the amplifier volumes were set, and Rick bored of rattling off random drum rolls. An electric charge of psychic energy hung in the air as the group prepared to make music together.

"Here's something I came up with," Joey said. "It's in E." He began playing a simple but effective four-chord punk rock riff, showing Clara his finger work. His fingers flew frantically up and down the neck of his guitar. The sound was raw and furious.

"I like it." Clara smiled and followed the root notes on her bass. As soon as she joined in, the sound became thicker and richer.

"Fast, catchy, and angry," Steve nodded in approval. "Not as hardcore as Minor Threat, but still good. Kinda sounds like the Pistols mixed with Nirvana. Keep playing." Steve started vocalizing. He used the lyrics he had written and experimented with melodies and phrasing. Rick tapped his sticks on his knees, learning the tune before starting in with a beat. When the drums did kick in, the song really took flight.

It was obvious to all four that the group had instant chemistry. Although the music was still sloppy and the singing a little wild and off-key, the energy and emotion they were able to channel into the sound was palpable and powerful. All members of the group were grinning widely as they worked on their first song together.

The hours flew by. By the time evening was upon them, the group had fleshed out the basic framework of three songs – three short sonic blasts of unbridled punk rock energy. They wrapped up their first session spent, satisfied, and eager to do it again.

"I'm sore as hell, but that was the most fun I have ever had," Rick said, rolling his shoulders. "I thought my arms were going to fall off during that last tune."

"You'll need to work on your stamina," Steve said. "We all do. We should practice again soon."

"Absolutely," Joey agreed. His fingertips were red,

raw, and throbbing. "We have just over a month until the show. Let's rehearse as often as possible."

"We need a name," Clara said. Uncharacteristically, she was still smiling.

"Yes we do," Steve said. "Start brainstorming. Come up with some ideas. We'll choose the best one."

Over the next few weeks, the group met almost every night in Rick's garage. All four were motivated, inspired, and totally committed to the project. A strong bond developed and it transcended music. Something special and nearly mystical united the four friends. They became a family.

In the insular high school environment, information traveled fast. It did not take long for word to get out that the four weirdest kids at TCI had started a band and that they planned to perform at the upcoming talent show. The gossip factory went into overtime production. In the popular cliques, the new group became a rich source of material for mockery. Even Steve, who had gained a certain grudging acceptance, found himself a target for an unusually hostile campaign of harassment in the weeks and days leading up to the show. The comments hurled at him and the others were sarcastic, childish, and vicious.

"Look! It's the rock star! Can I have your autograph?"

"Where's your groupies?"

"Punk sucks!"

"*You* suck!"

"You should call your band The Losers!"

"The Freaks!"

Steve was on his way to meet the others in the alcove when he heard that last one. He stopped cold, turned to face the origin of the insult, and smiled. "That is brilliant," he said. "Thank you!"

"I have the band name," Steve announced when he

reached the others already gathered in the alcove. He paused for dramatic effect.

"The Freaks."

And so it was. Joey, Rick, and Clara knew immediately that the name was perfect.

The Freaks continued their disciplined rehearsal schedule in the days leading up to the talent show. After their last practice session on the night before the show, they went for a walk around Rick's neighborhood. The anticipation was building. A nervous charge had the four members buzzing.

"I hope we don't suck," Rick muttered as they wandered through the dark.

"Don't say that," Steve said. "Don't even think that. You'll pysche yourself out. Think *positively*, dude."

"We won't suck," Joey said. "We've been practicing, getting tighter...getting *better*. Just get up there and have fun."

"We're going to blow minds and melt faces," Clara grinned. "I can't wait."

"What if people hate us?" Rick was worried.

"Who cares?" Steve said. "We have nothing to prove and nothing to lose. Do you really care what the drones think anyway? I don't. I just want to get up on that stage and unleash the fury."

"We just need to believe in ourselves," Joey said, "even if no one else does."

Walking with the group felt great. *We're like a little tribe,* Joey thought. *A gang, a family.* He was again aware of the beauty of his youth and the fantastic potential of the years ahead. Forming the musical group, creating something so pure and powerful, had given him a tremendous boost of confidence. It was simply punk rock music – he understood this – but the drive and imagination it had taken to conceive of and follow through with the project gave him faith in himself and in his ability to fashion his own future. He and the others had been empowered, liberated from the miasma of hopelessness.

The day of the talent show arrived. The show was to be held in the school auditorium, starting at 6 PM. The Freaks gathered with the rest of the performers backstage. They were scheduled to go on last. There was a sense among the organizers, students, and other acts that The Freaks were a joke. The school did not want to be embarrassed. Many parents were in attendance.

Joey, Steve, Rick, and Clara huddled together in the corner, anxious and self-conscious. The other performers, mainly dance acts, singers, and air band groups, were radiating hostile vibes. There was one other live band scheduled to perform – a heavy metal trio featuring Chad and Duane, the pool hall hooligans who had so courteously introduced Joey to the town of Tempest. They called their group Night Lightning. They would be opening the show.

Chad approached The Freaks, his Randy Rhodes model Flying V guitar already strapped on. He was fully decked out in his heavy metal stage regalia – he was a spandex, leather, and denim walking music video. "Are you weirdos actually going to desecrate that stage with your punk rock shit show?" he snarled.

"Freaks, not Weirdos," Steve corrected him.

"What is *that* thing?" Chad pointed at Joey's guitar.

"My axe," Joey deadpanned. "I use it to play hot licks and wicked riffs." Joey did an exaggerated Eddie Van Halen impression, fingers flailing, his face distorted in guitar ecstasy.

Chad was not amused. "What a piece of shit. Looks like you got it at K-Mart."

"Sears, I think," Joey said, "but I can still shred like

the pros on this bad boy." The sarcasm was lost on Chad.

"We're going to blow you off the stage," Chad said. "Major labels are fighting over Night Lightning. We're gonna get signed. We're gonna be famous."

Steve yawned. Clara giggled. Rick practiced twirling his drum sticks. Joey nodded. "Good for you," he said. "I"m sure you'll have all the money, coke, and groupies your little heart desires."

"Damn right," Chad said. "You better believe it." Chad walked away to wait with the other members of Night Lightning, playing guitar as he strutted.

"That's exactly what it's *not* about," Steve said. "Money, fame, whores, and drugs – that's all bullshit. Integrity, passion, creativity, and freedom – that's what I believe in. Those burnouts are conformists of the worst kind."

The show was about to begin. The emcee was on stage, warming up the audience with a comedy routine. When he was done he introduced the first act.

"Ladies and gentleman," the emcee announced. "Please welcome to the stage TCI's very own *Night Lightning!*" A generous round of applause, cheering, and whistling followed.

The lights were dimmed and the curtain went up. The techs had worked out an elaborate light show to accompany Night Lightning's performance. The trio launched into a cover of Metallica's *Master of Puppets* as a bright strobe pulsed. Blue and red spotlights swirled. The music was loud and thumping. The guitar and bass players banged their heads and swung their long hair in circles as they hammered away at their instruments. It was an intense display. The audience loved it.

When the first song crashed to a finish and while the

crowd was still in the delirious throes of exhilaration, Night Lightning charged into an Iron Maiden song. They were tight and well-rehearsed, a slick, polished act.

Backstage, The Freaks watched in amazement.

"They're pretty good," Rick observed.

"They can definitely play," Joey agreed.

"I'm actually impressed," Clara said.

"They sound like every other high school cover band," Steve shrugged.

Night Lightning finished their blistering spectacle of a set to the uproarious approval of the crowd. For the next few hours, dance acts, pop music, and air band routines dominated the stage, with a few magic acts and pet tricks thrown in for flavor. The Freaks waited anxiously backstage. Finally, the time came for them to perform.

The Freaks walked onstage. Joey and Clara plugged in their guitars. Rick got behind the provided drum kit. Steve approached the microphone. The emcee watched as they moved into position. The audience was silent, unsure of what to expect from the four misfits who stood before them. Dense, nervous energy hung in the air like suspended particulates. The tension was shattered by the clearly audible commentary of a heckler in the audience: "Losers with guitars. This should be entertaining."

The emcee ignored the comment and introduced the band: "This next act is a new group, and this is their debut performance. Please welcome to the TCI stage, *The Freaks!*" A sparse, but polite, smattering of applause followed.

"Hello," Steve said into the microphone. "This is a song we wrote. It's called *Mental Prison*. It's about conformity, society, and the importance of thinking for yourself." he glanced back at the others, nodded, and counted the song in with a shout: "1,2,3,4!" The band burst into their first tune.

For the next ten minutes, The Freaks blazed through five original songs, one after another, in a relentless sonic assault. They bounced, flailed, and rocked as they lost themselves in the music. They played even faster and more furiously than they had in practice, totally in the moment and completely present to the exuberant spirit of youth, which they channeled through their performance. It was a raw, magnificent expression of all the frustration and angst that had accumulated in their complicated teenage hearts. When the last chord was struck, the four musicians, sweating and breathing hard, nearly collapsed. The audience did not know what had hit them.

"Wow," someone near the front of the crowd said in the silent moment. As if on signal, the audience erupted in genuine, appreciative applause. It was an outpouring, an incredible release of emotion, as if the group onstage had tapped into the collective unconscious of the audience and opened the floodgates. The Freaks had given their all on the stage, with passion and sincerity. The music was rough and the musicians' abilities limited, but the audience was moved by the honest display of creativity they had just witnessed.

"Thank you!" Steve shouted into the microphone. The group walked off the stage happy.

Life moved on. The school year continued. The band played shows at local clubs and halls for the next year or so and developed a small, but loyal, following. They recorded an album on a rented four-track and released it independently. They planned to tour Canada and the US, but disbanded before this goal was achieved. The Freaks never got rich, never got famous, never even left Tempest, but they made an indelible impression on those who saw them play. Other groups were formed in their wake, inspired by the group's determination, enthusiasm, DIY ethos, and commitment to individuality.

As the world changed and the Information Age began, Joey, Steve, Rick, and Clara hurtled into adulthood, still grappling with domestic, academic, social, and emotional issues. Their struggles weren't over. Great unknown, unseen obstacles and challenges loomed in their futures. Life still had many surprises in store for the four friends. Playing in the band had, however, shaped their perspective on the world, and, though their paths would eventually diverge, they would always be, in their hearts, The Freaks.

The Traveler

In the great green room, there was a time machine, a lead suit, and a picture of the first man on the moon. The man in the lead suit was assisting another, the traveler, into the machine. The year was 1995. The traveler's destination was 25 years into the future.

Strapped in and secured, the traveler relaxed into his seat and prepared for the journey. He was excited, anxious, appropriately nervous, and absolutely thrilled by the expedition into the unknown upon which he was about to embark. This was to be the first Future Jump for his team. The machine had passed a rigorous testing phase, and the traveler had logged hundreds of hours in the simulator. It was now time for the initial human-piloted trial run.

The assistant in the lead suit exited the machine chamber and went to his terminal in the console room. All was going according to procedure. Mankind was on the threshold of an incredible new era. It was the dawning of the age of space/time mastery - a giant evolutionary leap. For reasons known only to his ultimate, mysterious superiors in the shadowy cabal that authorized, funded, and oversaw this mission, the traveler was being sent to a very specific time in the future. He could speculate, however – and he suspected that it had something to do with gathering information on a possible upcoming catastrophe.

Prediction and simulation software can only reveal so much about potential future scenarios. In order to obtain hard, usable data, one needs to be physically present to gather it. The traveler, recruited for his strength and stamina, as well as his mental fortitude, would be the individual who would cross the abyss, enter the brave new world of the next millennium, and gather this information.

The machine came to life, a rumbling, flashing, cacophonous beast of metal, glass, and wire. The traveler closed his eyes, held his breath, and gripped the arms of his seat. The walls of the chamber took on a shimmering, translucent appearance. Strange lights of indistinct color began to swirl around the machine. The traveler felt an unpleasant pressure building in his skull. A high-pitched wail rose within his ears. He thought maybe he was screaming, but he couldn't be sure. His mind was collapsing into a dissociative void...then, suddenly, silence, darkness, an eerie calm.

As if waking from a deep sleep, the traveler slowly regained consciousness. He was no longer inside of the machine. He was now seated on a bench on a large, busy street in a city of considerable size. Vehicles of makes and models he had never before seen zipped by him at a dizzying rate. Pedestrians, seemingly oblivious to his sudden appearance, walked up and down the sidewalk. He was exuberant. The machine had worked! If the engineers had gotten it right, he should now be in the year 2020. It was almost unfathomable.

The traveler took a moment to marvel at his surroundings, and the significance of what had just just transpired. He then began to do the job he had been trained for: diligently observing his environment and the people within it. His superiors would, no doubt, be interested in every little detail.

The traveler sat on the bench and scanned his immediate surroundings. He noticed a woman approaching. Her head was down and she walked slightly hunched over, her eyes on an object in her left hand. The object was some sort of device. The traveler could see it emitting a faint, green light. The woman was entirely captivated by the device, not once lifting her gaze as she approached. As the woman neared, the traveler was shocked to see that she was essentially naked. Two small, fabric skulls covered the nipples of her exposed breasts. She wore skimpy panties emblazoned with another large, leering human skull. On her feet she wore pink combat boots.

The traveler was astonished, but what really shocked him was what the woman had done to her face. Her nose and lips had been surgically altered to resemble those of a cat. Whiskers and black and orange stripes had been tattooed on her face. Were those cat ears poking through the brightly dyed hair on her head? The traveler watched her pass in abject disbelief.

A nasty smell caught his attention. He was able to pry his eyes away from the catwoman in search of the source of the stink. It was easy to find. Here now, following closely (too closely) behind the woman, was a vision directly out of a horror movie – a menacing, lumbering caricature of a villain. It was an absurd sight. The man was wearing a black leather trench coat embellished with spikes, chains, and animal bones. He wore a dirty, tattered top hat and carried a large staff with a human skull affixed to one end. It was not immediately apparent if the skull was real or not. The man's features were entirely obscured by a muddy, brown mask.

The stench grew as the man approached. The traveler realized that the man had a thick layer of human feces caked on his face. The man in the poop mask was obviously trying to intimidate those around him. He walked the street like a predator. As he passed the traveler, he lunged in his direction and sneered, revealing sharpened teeth and a modified tongue. The traveler could only stare, dumbfounded, as the ridiculous character walked up the street with an exaggerated, silly swagger, leaving a trail of excrement behind him.

The traveler took a moment to compose himself. He was only 25 years removed from his own time, but what little he had seen of this world was vastly, frighteningly, different. *These people seem so primitive*, he thought. *The technology appears to be sufficiently advanced, yet the populace has apparently regressed.* Everywhere he looked, he could see examples of this unexpected dichotomy.

The cars on the street were, to his eyes, appropriately futuristic, yet the drivers had the appearance of tribal throwbacks – hairy, unkempt, tattooed, near-nude, atavistic specimens with dull expressions on their slack faces. Fantastically sophisticated devices and high technology were abundant, yet all signs indicated an extremely anti-intellectual, escapist culture. Such a strange juxtaposition!

He noticed that many of the pedestrians who passed by were drinking the same beverage. He found an empty can on the ground at his feet. The garish writing on the over-sized can proclaimed the fluid inside to be Narconade, a potent mixture of chemicals promising "12 hours of bliss!" Across the street, a group of children were exiting a clinic. The sign above the door read "LobotoMart." The children were no more than 12 years old and each had a freshly sealed incision across his or her forehead. They were giggling, drooling, and stumbling down the street.

Above the clinic, a massive billboard announced an upcoming sporting event. The sign displayed animated depictions of graphic violence. Two uniformed teams of men were locked in brutal, close-quarters combat, stabbing, slicing, and disemboweling each other in an obscene display of carnage. Interspersed with these images were shots of deliriously excited, cheering spectators. The next game was scheduled for this very evening. The traveler was appalled. In his short stay, he had gathered enough information to provide a rather grim assessment of the near future to his superiors.

Despite his training and innate strength of mind, body, and spirit, the traveler was beginning to feel strongly uncomfortable – threatened, even – in this hostile, unfamiliar environment. He decided the best course of action would be to find a newspaper, collect as much data as he could from its pages, and then find a safe, quiet place to wait for the engineers to return him to his own time. He spotted a trashcan on the corner. He walked toward it calmly – confidently, attempting to attract as little attention as possible from the other pedestrians on the bustling street.

As the traveler neared the trashcan and prepared to inconspicuously examine its contents in search of a newspaper, he heard voices directly behind him. He quickly, reflexively spun around, ready to defend himself. There before him stood the LobotoMart children, each clutching a can of Narconade, their forehead incisions still oozing pink fluid. A few of them were pointing their mobile devices at him. *Were they filming this encounter?* he wondered. *Why?* Two of the larger children approached him, their black, lifeless eyes locked on his. They were vaguely grinning and leering at him like murderous idiots, breathing heavily from their open mouths.

The LobotoMart children closed in on the traveler. While a few stood back to record the assault, the rest began to strike in a disorganized, chaotic flurry of tiny arms and legs. Despite being half the size of their target, they were furiously aggressive and strangely fearless, like a pack off wild, rabid dogs. The traveler was forced to defend himself. He did so easily, using his training and considerable strength to fight off the feral children efficiently and systematically, until they were piled upon each other at his feet.

The traveler expected the rest to launch an attack, but they simply turned around and walked away unfazed, leaving their bloody and battered companions lying in a heap on the sidewalk. The other pedestrians paid no attention to the sudden violence. No one even looked up from their mobile devices.

The traveler was finally able to continue his search for a newspaper. He examined the trashcan and was not surprised to find it full of empty Narconade cans. There were, of course, no newspapers. For as far as he could see, in fact, there were no newsstands or newspaper vending machines.

There was a bookstore across the street, however, but according to the signage it specialized in pornography of the most lurid and perverse kind. The pictures displayed in the windows were revolting. *Do people even read anymore?* The traveler decided to continue on his way in search of a secluded spot to await his extraction.

He had not gone far when he heard a deafening roar above and behind him. Something was approaching with a thunderous din. He looked up and felt true fear for the first time since he had arrived. Hovering now, mere feet above his head, was a nightmarish contraption. It appeared to be a large, robotic flying machine held aloft by four powerful rotors. It was black and menacing, equipped with a variety of instruments and weapons. The traveler was utterly astonished. A high-pitched, ear-piercing metallic shriek promptly penetrated his head, driving away his thoughts and forcing him to his knees.

Pain and panic immobilized the traveler. The craft then emitted a thick, green mist, which completely enveloped him. His eyes burned. He gagged and frothed at the mouth.

He felt like a cockroach at the mercy of some omniscient, omnipotent exterminator. As his consciousness quickly ebbed away, he couldn't help but admire the extraordinary design and magnificent engineering of the machine.

The Curriculum

In some philosophies, it is believed that the whole of reality arises from our thoughts. There is nothing in this world that did not exist first as an idea. What we perceive as the external world is a reflection of our collective consciousness. In the beginning, before the word, was a *thought*, and that thought became action, action which created an entire universe. Human beings now inhabit the universe and possess, like the original, primordial force, powerful creative potential. The thoughts contained within each individual mind have the capacity to contribute to the formation of this world. For better or for worse, value-added or non-value-added, each of us participates in the co-creation.

In a possible alternate world, a war over the destiny of mankind is fought in the battlegrounds of the mind. One faction seeks to inhibit human development, the other seeks advancement of the species. Certain individuals, through a hard process of awakening and the occasional spontaneous revelation, become aware of their role in this conflict. Most people, however, live their lives in total, merciful ignorance, never suspecting that they are, by proxy, combatants in the war for the future.

Christopher Shepherd is one such man who lives in a state of blissful ignorance. Despite this ignorance, forces are moving around him. Spheres of influence are aligning, waves of change are converging upon him. Soon, the scales of sleep will fall from his eyes. Soon he will awaken to the harsh light of the truth.

Christopher is a first grade teacher at a small school in a suburban neighborhood. He is a middle-aged married father of two. He loves his family, enjoys his work, and is a generally congenial man with a positive attitude and an optimistic view of life. He gets along well with his coworkers, is liked and respected by his students, and is adored and admired by his family. In the evening, he and his wife, Lucy, walk the dog around their quiet neighborhood. On the weekend, the whole family enjoys leisure time together – baseball games, barbecues, board games, and movies. Christopher leads a remarkably typical middle-class life, but he is happy and fulfilled.

The day that his life changed course began like any other...with one exception: he had awoken from a dream that he would never forget. Over breakfast, Christopher made an attempt to share the dream with his wife.

"Had a weird one last night," he said casually, sipping his second cup of coffee. "I mean, wow! Not sure how to even describe it..."

He and his wife often shared their dreams with each other. She knew immediately what he was referring to. "Care to try?" she asked, genuinely curious.

"Well," said Christopher, taking a minute to gather his thoughts, "I was in a classroom, only I wasn't teaching. I was a student sitting at a desk. There were other people there, other adults...they were students, too. I was just sitting there, a little confused, but curious – I didn't know why I was in that room. Then the door opened, and in walked this strange-looking man. It's hard to explain, but somehow I knew he wasn't completely human. He sort of glowed with an electrical aura, like a ghost, or hologram...or *something*. Anyway, it was bizarre, but I wasn't frightened. I was actually in awe. I felt privileged, honored to be in his presence. This spectral man stood at the blackboard and started speaking to us. I can't recall his exact words, but he made me – and the others too, I'm sure – feel special, selected...like we had been recruited for a very important task or mission. I wish I could remember exactly what he said! It was amazing, profound stuff."

Christopher finished his coffee and looked deeply into Lucy's eyes, gauging her reaction to his dream. He continued:

"I feel like I was given tremendously valuable information – information of vital importance – but I can't recall anything specific. Anyway, the strange man looked directly at me, raised his arms, said 'Christopher, save the young minds!' and blasted me with bolts of electricity from his fingers. I woke up startled and I could actually feel my head tingling. Whew! What a dream."

Christopher exhaled, relieved. It felt good to share the weird dream – a dream that had actually left him a bit shaken and slightly disturbed. Lucy was now studying his face, clearly deep in thought. Christopher trusted her insights.

"Sounds to me like you are putting a lot of pressure on yourself to succeed," Lucy said. "You want to be a good teacher, a good role model. You have high expectations of yourself and your students. You fear failure, you fear letting down your students. You value education and are proud of the work you do, but you are an idealist with high standards. I think you need to be a little easier on yourself. You are a good teacher – and a good person! I think you had a stress dream."

Christopher thought about what Lucy had said before replying. "Hmm...you could be right. I do have that meeting with Principal Woodbeck this morning. I'm sure the dream is a reflection of my anxiety. It was a strange one, though. So *vivid*!"

The rest of the morning followed routine course. Christopher arrived at the school just before 8 AM. He went directly to the faculty lounge hoping to spend a few relaxing minutes reading the paper and perhaps catching up on gossip before his meeting with Woodbeck.

As usual, the lounge was full of teachers. On a typical morning, one would find a variety of moods on display – some teachers arrived for work eager, alert, and enthusiastic about their jobs, others were less than thrilled. A few jaded souls had grown to strongly dislike what they did for a living and would rather be anywhere else. Some teachers, Christopher suspected, actually hated children and tragically chose the wrong profession. On this day, Christopher could instantly perceive a certain excited buzz in the air as he entered. *Some juicy gossip going 'round*, he thought.

Christopher took a seat on a sofa, picked up a newspaper from the coffee table, and listened to the chatter. There were 15 or so teachers in the room, all talking at once in an animated frenzy. It became clear that most were talking about meetings they had had with Principal Woodbeck, meetings in which, undoubtedly – just like the meeting scheduled for Chris that very morning – school policy and protocol had been discussed. Apparently, some rather substantial changes were being implemented. Not being fully cognizant of the facts, Christopher stayed quiet and simply listened.

Linda Hashtieg, a fifth grade teacher fresh out of college and full of youthful enthusiasm, was speaking: "I think the new curriculum is simply fantastic. It's about time the education system emerged from the Stone Age and embraced the modern world. The classical academic model is stagnant and archaic...not to mention sexist, racist, and totally outdated. We need to teach children tolerance, equality, and acceptance."

Linda spoke with passion and conviction. Many of the other teachers were vehemently nodding their heads in agreement. Linda's words were, to Christopher's ears, vaguely positive, but somehow devoid of real meaning. Her words did not sit well with him, and as the conversation progressed, he began to feel even more uncomfortable.

"We need to free the impressionable young minds from the tyrannical influence of their parents," said Albert Genda, a curmudgeonly old teacher nearing retirement. "Children learn by example and I can tell you from years and years of experience, that what goes on in some of their homes is downright appalling. Some of those parents are not fit to raise children. They simply can't be trusted. It is our duty, as educators, to counteract the negative influence of the family unit. It is imperative that we prepare them for the real world by carefully redefining and clarifying their values."

Al was highly respected by his peers. They listened reverently as he spoke. Christopher was skeptical, but paid close attention.

"What we do in these hallowed halls will reverberate through history," Al said. "Through the meticulous molding of these young minds, we are creating a bold and bright future. As teachers, we are agents of change. The new curriculum is a true innovation in education."

When Al finished his short but impassioned speech, the room was quiet. The other teachers sat in contemplative silence, as if they had just been addressed by a sage of great wisdom and authority. Christopher was less impressed. He was, in fact, rather disturbed. The room had taken on the mood of a meeting of revolutionary zealots. The new curriculum apparently had a great effect on the faculty.

Christopher quietly excused himself and left the room. He decided to wait out the rest of the time before the morning meeting with Principal Woodbeck in his empty classroom. He could organize his teaching materials and perhaps clean up a bit before the kids arrived.

As Chris made his way down the hall toward the classroom, an uncanny, inexplicable feeling of dread washed over him. The familiar halls of the school now felt ominous, alien – even dangerous. He was suddenly filled with acute anxiety.

He finally reached the classroom. He unlocked the door and slipped into the darkened room before becoming overcome with vertigo. Leaning against the wall, he took a few deep breaths and calmed himself. *That dream*, he thought. *That's why I feel so weird. That dream spooked me.* Recognizing the probable source of his anxiety, he relaxed. He reached over and flicked the light switch.

The illuminated room revealed an unexpected sight – on each desk sat a large computer monitor. They had not been there the day before.

"What is this?" Christopher muttered. He walked over to the closest desk, feeling confused and slightly dazed. Large headphones were perched atop each monitor. Each of the monitors displayed the same words and images, all apparently connected to a central computer. The computer was running a software program of what appeared to be the new curriculum. Christopher could see the subjects listed on each screen:

Gender Identification
Teen Sexuality
Drugs and Alcohol
Apps and Devices
Video Game Appreciation
The Art of the Selfie
Pop Culture
Violence in Society
Death Ed

There were many more subjects of a wildly disparate assortment. The list was extensive and all-encompassing, touching on virtually every aspect of life and the human experience...except academics.

The software was designed like a video game and Christopher figured that a virtual reward system of pleasing sounds and images had been included to fully immerse the children in the program.

This is Pavlovian conditioning, Christopher realized. *Pure brainwashing.*

Conspicuously missing from the list of subjects were those of the traditional variety: math, science, literature, history, geography, etc. Christopher was truly alarmed now. *Is this a deliberate attempt to dumb down our children? What purpose do teachers serve in this new system? Why wasn't I told about this?*

Christopher realized that the time for his meeting was rapidly approaching. He had better get moving if he didn't want to be late. *Woodbeck will explain,* he thought optimistically. *I'm sure there's a good reason for all this.*

Christopher had a hard time accepting that such drastic changes were being made. He had a hard time believing that those in the upper levels of the system would deliberately sabotage the future. He had a strong sense that there was something just beneath the surface that he could neither see nor understand.

Mr. Woodbeck's office was just down the hall from Christopher's classroom. He arrived right on time for the meeting. After checking in with the receptionist, he took a seat and waited to be summoned. In the chair outside the principal's office, he felt like a kid who'd been caught doing something naughty or nasty. He felt as if he were awaiting judgment and punishment.

Christopher tried to shake the feeling by engaging the receptionist in small talk. "Busy day?" he asked her. There was no response. She appeared to be ignoring him.

"A lot of changes happening around here," Christopher said with a forced smile. "Things are sure different than when I was a kid!"

The receptionist looked up from her computer screen and glared at him. "Yes," she said. Her gaze locked on his and Christopher was startled by the cold, lifeless quality of her dark eyes.

"Mr. Woodbeck will see you now," the receptionist said. Christopher got up without saying anything and entered Woodbeck's office.

Inside, the room was dim and surprisingly chilly. Woodbeck was seated behind his desk, his stern, austere face partially in shadow and partially illuminated by the orange light of a small lamp. Woodbeck had the appearance of a mob boss, or an intelligence agency interrogator.

"Christopher, it's good to see you," Woodbeck said. "How have you been?" His eyes radiated the same cold intensity as the receptionist's.

"Good, thank you," Christopher replied, "but to be honest, I'm a little nervous about this meeting...and a little concerned about all the changes to the school and the curriculum."

"Yes, I suspected you would be. Significant changes have been implemented. The program has been activated and now the next phase is upon us. Our plan for the future requires all participants to work together as a cohesive unit. We must be on the same page, of the same mind. Do you understand?"

"I'm not sure," Christopher responded meekly. "I'm a little confused, actually. Could you please elaborate?"

"Potential resisters must be identified. Those who

cling to traditional values and modes of thinking *must be identified.*"

Something bizarre was happening. As Christopher watched, Mr. Woodbeck's body began to emit an eerie, red-hued light – he was suddenly glowing with an otherworldly electrical aura. Christopher could see sparks jumping and crackling and could smell a strong odor of ozone. He became terrified as Mr. Woodbeck spoke again, his voice now echoing in a way that made it sound as if it were being channeled from another dimension:

"*You* have been identified as a potential resister." Woodbeck raised his hands slowly, threateningly.

Bright sparks began to fly as the aura around Woodbeck increased in intensity. A moment's pause...and then, from outstretched fingers, Woodbeck directed fiery red bolts of energy at Christopher's head. A brief instant of agony, a ripping sound of skull-shattering volume, a timeless moment of panicked, flailing disorientation...and then Christopher transitioned into another realm of consciousness.

He awoke, heart palpitating and drenched in sweat, in his bed at home. His wife, Lucy, was beside him. Warm shades of red and orange were just beginning to fill the early morning bedroom. Christopher's relief was great. He felt as if his dream within a dream had revealed a frightening truth. He understood now, more than ever, that being a teacher was more than simply a job – in his occupation, he played a vital role in shaping the future through what he taught the children. He felt as if, through his dreams, he had been enlisted to serve humanity in a secret, but very real, war. Words flowed through his head: *The whole of reality arises from our thoughts. There is nothing in this world that did not exist first as an idea...*"

The Crucible

Awareness – not instantaneous, but gradual, an awakening of the senses guided by unseen forces. That is what occurred in Jason's life. He became aware of the game and his role within it through a slow, steady process of discovery. He had not set out on the journey deliberately. His transition from the waking dream state into the reality of his true existence had been activated without his knowledge or consent.

The situation was revealed to him through a series of apparently random and coincidental events - anecdotes and encounters which showed him that the life he thought he was living was largely an illusion. He came to realize that at some time in his past, perhaps at birth, he had been selected to participate in a sinister project. The dawning of his awareness came when he started to experience an unprovoked series of subtle attacks on his psyche.

The relentless harassment began mysteriously and rather suddenly. In the beginning, Jason had had no idea why he had been targeted, or by whom. What he had grown to accept, though, was that he was the subject of a cruel and bizarre campaign, the goal of which appeared to be the complete collapse of his mind and spirit. If the perpetrators had simply wanted him dead, he would have already been taken out. No, the agenda was much darker.

The first hint that he was the subject of a secret program came while Jason was enjoying a quiet, solitary evening of reading in his apartment. Jason studied philosophy at a large university. He has an appreciation for the world of ideas and concepts, and has always felt most comfortable being left alone with his thoughts. While

contemplating Spinoza's concept of an immanent God, a loud
noise from the apartment upstairs broke his concentration.

Wham! Bang! CRASH! It sounded as if someone was
destroying furniture directly above his head. It was so loud
and sudden that Jason actually jumped in his seat. It was
unusual to hear anything coming from that apartment, let
alone such a violent racket.

Quiet again, then *bang! Smash!* It was startling.
"What are they *doing* up there?" Jason said aloud. He made
an attempt to regain his composure and return his attention to
his studies. Within a few minutes he was once again lost in
the world of abstract concepts. It was a lovely place to be.

Bang! Bang! BANG!

"Oh, *come on!*" Jason said, his frustration building.
"This is ridiculous." He could feel his heart rate increasing.
His hands began to tremble. *They're doing that on purpose*,
he thought. *Why?* The idea was irrational – and slightly
paranoid. Jason decided to take a break from his studies. It
was futile to continue.

With quick, deft motions he snatched up the remote
control that was resting, as always, at his side. He powered
on his large, flatscreen television and the room was instantly
filled with the light and sound of typical evening
programming. A popular detective show was on the air, the
bland actors and uninspired sets were familiar and
comforting. A man and a woman stood on a rainy, late-night
street, discussing the body lying at their feet. The dialogue
was formulaic and predictable. Jason let his mind lapse into a
TV-trance.

"Poor kid. Such a bright future ahead of him," said
the male actor playing the part of grizzled veteran detective.
"Any ID?" he asked his female partner, who was looking
through the dead man's wallet. She pulled out a laminated
card. "Looks like our victim is...*was*...a university student,"

she said. "Name: Jason Durant."

Jason Durant – that was *his* name.

The world ceased for one infinitesimally small and surreal moment. Reality briefly skipped a beat like a damaged record. Jason's mind struggled to process what he had just heard. *Or had he?* His trance broken, he sat up and tuned his attention fully to the program.

"Looks like this kid's studyin' days are over," said the male detective. "He seems like a decent, clean-cut kid. Not obviously a drug user or criminal. I wonder what got him whacked."

The female detective broke the fourth wall and looked directly at the camera. "Don't worry, Jason. We'll find your killer," she said.

The station cut to a commercial. Before the announcer could launch into his insipid pitch, Jason powered off the television.

Whoa. That was really weird – too *weird,* he thought. *What a wild coincidence.*

At that moment, he could hear activity in the hall outside his door – footsteps and chatter. A group of people were noisily approaching his apartment. Their conversation was loud, raucous, and indistinct. At the precise instant in which they were in front of his door, a phrase spoken by a man in the group was clearly audible: "Only losers spend their nights alone, reading." Phony and exaggerated laughter followed, echoing down the hall. The group continued past Jason's apartment, the rest of the conversation lost to his ears.

Well, they couldn't have been talking about me, Jason thought. It was still more than a little disconcerting. The night was beginning to take on a dreamlike quality. *A walk, that's what I need. Fresh air, a clear mind.*

Jason put on his shoes and jacket and exited the apartment building, his destination: the convenience store on the corner of his block. The night air was invigorating. On this comfortably cool autumn evening, the sky was a rich shade of navy blue. The moon seemed unusually large, suspended above his head like an ominous sentinel, a night watchman observing Jason's sojourn on this strange evening.

Walking briskly, Jason allowed his mind to digest what he had just experienced. It was as if he had been suddenly thrust into a parallel dimension, an alternate version of the world that he normally occupied. He was not a drug user, as the detective character in the TV program had correctly observed, but he was starting to feel like he had been dosed with a powerful hallucinogenic.

Reason, he told himself. *Reason your way through this. There must be a rational answer.*

A semblance of sanity returned. The walk was working well – Jason was starting to feel much better. As he neared the convenience store, he happened to glance toward the street as a dark SUV was passing. There was a man leaning out of the front passenger window of the vehicle. He was looking straight at Jason, his features distorted in a grotesque scowl. "Fuck *yoooouuuu!*" the man yelled as the SUV accelerated and drove off.

The street was empty, the night silent. Jason could only stand there, confused and upset. *Who was that? Why me?* He was so disturbed he decided to forego his visit to the convenience store and instead turned and went back home. He wanted nothing more than to hide and, if possible, find refuge in the oblivion of sleep. He crawled into bed and soon found it. In this way, the first day of his awakening ended.

Jason's life was never the same. It was not long before he was fully immured in the game, a captive in its invisible confines, an unwilling contestant, an oblivious test subject. Strange incidents and disturbing coincidences became routine. It was as if the entire world was in on the joke...except for him.

Within a week of the first night of experiences, new neighbors moved into the apartment beside Jason, a group of students roughly his age. Before he had a chance to get to know them, or even introduce himself, they began to harass him, always in a subtle, covert way, always leaving room for that small voice inside Jason to ask, *Am I being paranoid?*

Sound assaults were a common tactic. At all hours of the day and night, but most particularly when he was trying to sleep, someone would begin banging on the walls. It always happened abruptly. Jason would be lying in bed, drifting off to sleep, when suddenly the silence would be shattered by an explosion of bangs and crashes, followed by eerie, maniacal laughter. A period of quiet would follow, and then, just as he was falling back to sleep, *WHAM!* It would happen all over again.

Jason ignored the noise for many days, choosing to believe that he was simply too sensitive, and that the walls were thin. Besides, if they *were* trying to disturb him, Jason reasoned, a hostile reaction from him is exactly what they would want. Jason made a valiant attempt to remain calm, but the relentless, chronic nature of the chaos soon eroded his ability to withstand it.

Sleep became a rare commodity. Jason lost his appetite and his weight dropped drastically. His mind ceased to function fully. The 'attacks' became overt, obvious, and undeniable. People marched up and down the hall outside of his apartment constantly, offering barely concealed commentary on his predicament. Jason overheard snatches of conversation from the faceless and nameless:

"...*someone* hasn't slept in days...hahaha...."

"Take a shower...you *stink!*"

"Asshole!" This particular insult was accompanied by a kick to his door.

For reasons not yet clear, the neighbors despised him. Jason simply could not understand what he had done to attract such negative attention. He had never spoken to them and had only ever had brief encounters in the halls or on the street, during which they rarely showed any emotion. In person, they appeared totally ambivalent toward him. It was all so bizarre.

The internet was a portal to the abyss and a window into the emerging nightmare that Jason inhabited. Online, the harassment was severe. There was no escape. It didn't take long for Jason to realize that he was being stalked at all times by a mysterious, malevolent, and very organized group. His activity was constantly tracked, his email accounts compromised.

In the early days of the 'program,' he had occasionally attempted to escape into the mindless entertainment of online games. The perpetrators were always waiting, ready to taunt, ready to torment. The modus operandi was always the same – subtle harassment, never too obvious, never specific. 'They' would reveal themselves using passive-aggressive hints and loaded intimations.

In an email to one of his few remaining friends, Jason had mentioned, as an aside, that he had given up smoking and was considering joining a gym. Later that day he went online to play a role-playing game he enjoyed. Almost immediately, words and phrases related to what he had written in his email began appearing on screen as in-game chat between other players.

"Need a smoke?"

"How many reps did you do today?"

"Work out!"

These seemingly innocuous comments were never directed at him specifically, but were charged with hostile intent. Jason quickly learned to ignore the chatter and for a while, he was determined to try and have fun in the game, regardless of whether or not he was being stalked. This proved difficult. His character was, invariably, hunted down and killed each time he ventured forth into the game world. It was exasperating and disheartening, a disturbing reflection of what he was experiencing in his regular existence.

In the comments sections of news articles and videos, in message board postings, and anywhere user-generated content was supported, Jason found references to his life and to his predicament. Were the stalkers human? Was he perhaps the target of super strong and ultra-malicious AI? His imagination started to consider some truly extraordinary possibilities.

The internet, once a source of entertainment and escape, transformed into an exaggerated virtual corollary to what Jason was experiencing in his day-to-day existence.

There was no escape.

Disheveled and distraught, Jason sat alone in his apartment for days. He once uttered a short phrase to himself while sitting on his couch in the dark, late one sleepless night: "Is this hell?" When he was next able to summon the strength of spirit to leave the relative safety of his small apartment, new graffiti adorned the walls of the hall:

THIS IS HELL

Jason was not completely surprised to see the words painted in gaudy, bright red in a spot in which he was sure to see them. He had come to expect exactly this sort of thing, though it was impossible to ignore, and the familiar thoughts again filled his head, *Is this a coincidence? A message directed at me? Am I going crazy?*

It became harder and harder for Jason to live a normal life. People glared at him on the street. His fellow students at the university inexplicably ostracized him. The professors graded him unfairly. He stopped attending classes and eventually, even his family distanced themselves, refusing to answer his calls. It all seemed to happen at once, in an avalanche of ill fortune and social failure. Within a few months, he transformed into a depressed pariah, totally isolated, and on the verge of physical and emotional collapse.

Jason started to rely on sleeping pills and powerful sedatives obtained from a variety of sources. Narcotics offered relief...for a while, at least. Soon, though, even *they* could not hide the hideous nature of his existence. In fact, the drugs started to have an extremely adverse effect on him. The more he consumed, the more he broke with reality...and his grip was already tenuous.

While under the influence, Jason began communicating with his perceived tormentors. (Or did he?) His pill consumption increased and his subconscious began manifesting its paranoid persecution fantasies. He heard children outside his window mocking him. He addressed them from the depths of a dissociative fugue.

"I know you're there! I know what you are doing! I will persevere. I will survive! You can't break me!" He could hear the children laughing. He opened the window, ready to confront them. It was somehow night, though he hadn't noticed the day slip away.

"Come here! Talk to me!" *Was that them? On the other side of the street now, hiding in the shadows? How did they get there so fast?* "Cowards!"

He shut the window and resumed pacing his now filthy, cluttered, unsanitary apartment. Moments later he could hear the children. They were at his window again, throwing pebbles at the glass and giggling. Jason ran back to the window and threw it open as quickly as he could, determined to catch them in the act.

The night was still. The children had disappeared. *Unless...wait, is that them?* Jason could see indistinct forms silhouetted against the pale yellow glow of a streetlight just up the street. "I see you!" he yelled. "*I SEE YOU!*" Maniacal laughter. Was it his?

Jason lost track of time, in a very real and literal sense. There was nothing to distinguish one day or night from the next. He was a passenger in his own life, carried by the tide in a hazy stupor. High strangeness increased. He was now a fully activated shadow persona. This was revealed to him, mercifully, one night while in the throes of a drug-induced state of psychosis.

He was engaged in an intense, philosophical conversation with a room full of guests, passionately defending his position on some now forgotten topic. Animated dialogue and friendly, excited discourse rang in his ears and filled his head with a pleasant, warm sensation. He was in his element, thoroughly enjoying himself...and then something *changed.*

One moment he was speaking to the gathering, and the next moment he was sitting alone on his couch. The sound of voices reverberated in his ears, but the room was totally empty. It was as if the people he had been speaking to had suddenly simply faded away. He was confused, disconcerted, and embarrassed. Had he been talking to himself the entire time?

The fragility of his psyche and his loose grip on reality frightened him deeply. Jason could sense the gaping maw of total insanity waiting in the near future, ready to consume him. *I'm in danger,* he thought. *Something's wrong.*

At that exact moment, a blaring horn from a car passing by on the street seemed to confirm his thoughts. Of course, Jason's sensitivity to coincidental occurrences was high, but the timing of the sound was suspicious. Jason could feel the very nature of his personality rupturing, as if micro-tears were forming on the fabric of his soul.

I'm scared, he thought. *I need help.* Again, at that very moment, another car passed by his window, horn blaring – *HONNNNKK!* Doppler Effect distorted the sound into the shriek of a demented banshee as the car sped away. In the deepest, secret recesses of his wounded heart, he *knew* the sounds were directed at him. His thoughts were being accessed and read in real time. It altered the nature of the game.

For the first time since Jason's life began to fall apart – or, as he now understood, came under attack, he wept. He cried like he had never cried before. It was an incredibly intense release of emotion. Water flowed from his eyes as if he had tapped into the primordial ocean of pre-creation. He wept, and gradually, a sense of peace washed over him. Jason was purging. He was on the verge of a real breakthrough.

I need to talk to somebody, Jason thought. A random passing car honked in reply. "I need to make changes," he said out loud, his courage building. In that moment, though he wasn't fully conscious of it, he made a pact with himself. This was *his* life, and his alone. It was time to regain control. Although he might never understand the exact nature of what was happening to him, he was now determined to fight for his mind, his soul, and his very existence. From beyond the veil, his spirit was speaking to him.

Jason looked around his apartment and allowed the truth of the current state of his life to pass into his awareness. The apartment was a disaster. Dust and filth covered every surface. Empty junk food containers and pill bottles were piled up in every corner. The debris and detritus of a shattered mind completely covered the floor. Jason realized how far he had slipped away, and it was shocking.

"It ends now," he vowed.

Jason was shaking off the effects of the pills. His head was clearing, his mind awakening. Hope was mending his now resilient heart. "No more drugs," he said. Nascent determination strengthened his resolve to face the myriad challenges ahead.

It was then that Jason embraced his role as a target. The goals now were to find out who the perpetrators were and to discover the purpose of the game and why he had been selected. His newfound confidence and optimism could not prepare him for what he was about to discover. The nature of the game was even stranger than he could have imagined.

"You are not alone." The words reached Jason in the same way that the other peculiar messages had – unexpectedly and perfectly timed. With fresh vigor and a renewed spirit, he set out on a mission to discover the truth. The internet proved to be his ally during this phase. To Jason's shock and wonder, there was an entire online subculture related to what he had been experiencing.

The information seemed to find Jason. With nothing other than the intention of finding the truth, he suddenly stumbled upon a dark, shadowy world of targeted individuals, perpetrators, stalking, and harassment, all linked to what appeared to be a program or campaign, the purpose of which was unknown and hotly debated. What was clear to Jason, though, is what he found written at the top of a website devoted to the topic:

You are not alone.

With those four, simple words, Jason's healing and his

true journey began. There was a vast amount of information online, much of it conflicting and contradictory, but Jason had learned to trust his intuition. It had guided him from the brink of collapse to the threshold of rebirth. He could also sense the presence of invisible benevolence – a spiritual midwife, as it were, assisting in the process.

He discovered, to his amazement, that there were many people going through the same thing he was...and not all of them were making it through. Some, however, were surviving, thriving, and were changed in a profound and positive way.

Jason spent a night immersed in the literature, visiting as many websites as he could find on the topic and gathering a plethora of data. There were many varied opinions on the nature of the 'game' and its true purpose. Jason kept his mind open and used his heart as a compass as he navigated the dark labyrinth.

Theories of all varieties, from the mundane to the supernatural, were discussed, debated, and vehemently defended or conversely attacked. There were those who firmly believed that the government and military were the perpetrators, using low frequency electromagnetic waves to assault the brains of targets, with the intent of driving the subjects totally, irrevocably insane.

Jason found the online journal of one such believer. This individual, who called himself Vigilant Patriot, described his harrowing experiences in vivid detail. "I am the victim of electronic warfare," he wrote. "The government is using voice-to-skull technology to fill my head with negative thoughts and to deprive me of sleep. They are trying to make me crazy. They are trying to break my mind and my will to live. No one believes me, of course. My friends and family have all abandoned me. This is exactly what 'They' want."

"I believe I was targeted because I pose a threat to them," the writer continued. "I am an active opponent of the New World Order. My blogs and podcasts reveal the truth of their plans for world domination. Now I am issuing a new warning: *You are next.*"

Jason was startled by Vigilant Patriot's description of high-tech psychological warfare, but he couldn't simply dismiss the account as the ravings of a paranoid lunatic. His own experiences had been truly bizarre, and he could relate to the feeling that it was near impossible to tell friends and family what was happening. It was too far-out for most people to believe.

An intriguing possibility being discussed referred to a top secret recruitment program initiated by the CIA, KGB, or some underground, undisclosed, rogue intelligence agency with no national allegiance and a hidden agenda.

There was also a faction of 'Experiencers' who felt that they were simply the targets of an organized group of anonymous, malcontent hackers who stalked and harassed them for pure enjoyment. Jason knew this to be somewhat true, but as a whole, this simplistic scenario was unsatisfactory and did not adequately explain the high-strangeness he and many others had encountered.

A growing group of targets were starting to uncover evidence that the game was being played on a higher dimensional level, perhaps even a spiritual level. This would explain some of the supernatural, apparently paranormal aspects of what the targeted individuals were experiencing. This was the perspective Jason could identify with most. It was an intuitive insight. In his growing awareness, the world began to appear much differently than it had before the program had begun. He seemed to be undergoing an awakening, as were many others. It was an amazing process.

During his random walk exploration, Jason found a video. It was titled *Spiritual Guidance for Targeted Individuals*, and it featured a beautiful, mysterious woman speaking articulately about the subject. She spoke with confidence and a deep understanding of what he and the other subjects of the strange game were experiencing.

"The process of ascension is painful," she said. "By now, I'm sure many of you have experienced a wide spectrum of emotions, running the gamut from despair to elation. That is to be expected and welcomed, if possible. You have been unplugged, awakened, *called.* The world you thought you inhabited is an illusion. I am here to help you graduate to the next level."

It all sounded a little 'new-agey' to Jason, but he was intrigued. It was an interesting premise that appealed to his sense of adventure...and, of course, his ego. It made him feel as if he were part of something larger than himself. It made him feel selected, special.

It was also, perhaps, too good to be true. What about those who hadn't made it through? What about those who were driven to the brink of destruction? What about those who had descended into total madness, or worse? What about those who had lost all hope and took their own lives? Had *they* been on the path to ascension?

The flood of information – and disinformation – pouring into into Jason's head was overwhelming. All that data, all those theories – it was too much to process. Jason could sense that pursuing the truth from a purely research-driven perspective could be a dangerous path to take. The internet was a treacherous brier patch to navigate.

Inconsistency, contradiction, deception...it was a virtual road to madness.

Connect with others, his heart spoke to him. *Connect with nature.* He needed to taste reality. He yearned to bathe in the radiance of the sun, and to breathe fresh, open air. He yearned for companionship and new experience. He yearned to live in harmony with his environment and his fellow human beings. Early in the morning after he had spent an entire night researching on the internet, he fixed his gaze on the door of his apartment and prepared to pass through the portal and re-enter the world of the living.

A week had passed since Jason last left his apartment. It had been many more days than that since his last conversation with a 'real' person. The idea of leaving his cave and facing the world outside filled him with anxiety, but he felt compelled to take a leap of faith and step into the morning light of a new realm – a new life, if he wanted it, which waited for him just beyond the gate.

It was 7 AM on a crisp, autumn day, and the world outside was illuminated in golden light. The expansiveness of the realm beyond the walls of Jason's apartment, his prison for the last few months, was disorienting. He felt vulnerable standing in the open, his body fragile, his very soul open to attack from every direction. *Agoraphobia*, he realized. Recognition brought relief.

Jason's eyes passed over the objects and details of a neighborhood that was once familiar to him, but which now seemed alien. The homes and landscaping hadn't changed, but it was as if a filter had been removed. Everything was brighter, clearer, more *substantial.* Jason's interior world had undergone a similar transformation. His mind, too, felt brighter and clearer, his spirit, his very *existence,* more substantial. *I'm alive,* he thought.

Awake.

The sensation of being connected to something much larger than himself was hard to dismiss. The game was still being played, Jason knew, but a new phase had begun. He walked the early morning streets of his city in search of *something.*

He spotted a coffee shop that he used to frequent. Memories of sipping a warm beverage and reading his books on philosophy returned to him in vivid detail. *A student,* he thought. *That's what I was. That's what I AM.* He was drawn, compelled, to enter the shop. He did.

It was quiet and welcoming inside. The smell of fresh coffee greeted him like an old friend. Early morning patrons smiled as he entered. *Newspapers, donuts, warm, inviting drinks. Hospitality, serenity.* Jason inventoried the rush of pleasant feelings. It was uplifting – a panacea, a pure elixir for the soul.

"Good morning!" the woman behind the counter said. "What can I get you?"

"Hello," Jason replied. It was the first word he had uttered to another person in the flesh in longer than he could remember. It was thrilling and a little frightening. "I'll have a medium coffee," he said, his anxiety diminishing quickly.

Jason's coffee was served and he took it to an empty seat at a table by the window. The sun was now fully up, the golden light transitioning into the purer white of midday. There was something magical about sitting in the coffee shop on a typical morning with the other regular customers. Electric romance fluttered in his heart. *This is good,* he thought.

Open to whatever the universe had in store for him, ready for adventure, and genuinely excited about the future, Jason enjoyed his existence. The coffee was tasty, the atmosphere in the shop perfectly suited to his current temperament. The people around him chatted quietly, discussing politics, sports, and popular entertainment. Some read newspapers, others sat in silence. Life happened.

The door of the shop opened, and in *she* walked.

I know her, Jason thought, before real recognition even entered his brain. It was instinctual. The woman walked right past his seat and marched up to the counter. She had dark hair, expressive (though somewhat sad) eyes, a small build, and a serious demeanor. *Where do I know her from?* Jason wondered. He tried not to stare, but he was thoroughly captivated.

"Good morning!" the lady behind the counter exclaimed. "What can I get you?"

"Medium coffee, please," the young woman said. The sense of the surreal returned. It was like deja vu, only much more intense. *I dreamed this,* Jason thought. *She's going to talk to me.*

She did.

As the dark-haired, strangely familiar woman walked past with her fresh coffee, she happened to glance in Jason's direction. "Hi," she said, a smile appearing on her naturally kind and pretty face. She stopped and looked at him quizzically. "Where do I know you from?"

Jason was momentarily stunned. Nervous energy coursed through his veins. He felt like an awkward prepubescent boy talking to a girl for the first time. He wasn't totally inexperienced with women, but there was an instant, powerful dynamic between he and the woman. Electromagnetic discharges arced from dimension to dimension. "Oh," he stammered, "I'm not sure. Have we met before?"

Just like that, the universe blinked an eye, and with a

beat of its infinite heart, the connection was made.

Jason recognized the importance of the encounter. Intuition practically screamed at him: *Talk to her! Don't miss your opportunity!*

"Are you a student?" Jason asked. "Maybe we had a class together."

"Hmm, no," she replied. "I'm actually new to town. Just moved here a few months ago. You seem so *familiar*, though! Weird." The woman took a step toward the door, reluctantly – an uncanny attraction worked its magic.

"Care to have a seat?" Jason offered her a chair. Why not? He had nothing to lose.

A twinkle of amusement flashed in the woman's eyes. She was flattered and intrigued. "Sure," she said. "I've got some time before my appointment."

She sat down across from Jason. The very air seemed to vibrate as electric currents passed between them across the small table.

"My name is Jason," he said, extending a hand. "Mary," the woman said as she shook his hand and completed the circuit. "It's nice to meet you."

Jason had never really developed a skill for small talk, but being in Mary's company was so comfortable and easy. Ostensibly, this was a first meeting, but Jason felt more as if he was being reunited with an extremely old friend after eons of separation – perhaps lifetimes.

"This is my favorite place to come for coffee," Jason said. "When I was in school I practically *lived* here. How about you, been here before?"

"A few times," Mary nodded. "It's good coffee...*strong* coffee...which I need today. I have an appointment, and I want to be alert and ready."

"Oh? Where is that?"

"Well, to be honest, it's with a psychiatrist," Mary

answered without hesitation. This level of candor was unusual for her, but Jason made her feel safe.

"I'm sorry. It's none of my business. I didn't mean to be so nosy."

"That's fine," Mary smiled. "I don't really have anything to hide. I only recently started seeing a psych. I've been going through some...stuff."

Mary gazed into her coffee cup, watching the deep, brown fluid swirling hypnotically. She had only ever spoken to her doctor about her recent difficulties. "It's hard to talk about."

"I understand. I really didn't mean to pry."

"No, it's okay. It actually feels pretty good to talk to someone else about it...someone who won't immediately want to drug me up or dismiss me as loony. I'm not, you know – crazy, that is. I've just been experiencing some really strange things."

Although she had held Jason's attention since the moment she had walked into the coffee shop, Jason was now fully, completely, undeniably absorbed in what she was saying. His eerie sensation of being in a dream intensified.

"You may not believe me," Jason said. "But I can relate."

Behind the scenes, wheels were turning. The machinations of destiny were in full operation, drawing these two individuals closer to each other and to their shared future.

Before he had time to think about what he was about to say, Jason stated, "I think we've been brought together for a reason." He said the words with confidence and a conviction that surprised even him. "Would you like to go for a walk with me?"

"My appointment..."

"Skip it," Jason insisted without missing a beat.

Mary – an intelligent, perceptive, sensitive, and cautious woman – heard, or rather *perceived,* an inner voice speaking: *Follow your heart,* it whispered. "That doctor is a fool anyway," she said. "A walk sounds like a good idea."

Soon, Jason and Mary were walking side by side on the mid-morning streets, both enjoying the quiet comfort in the presence of the other. Traffic was picking up as more and more people began driving to work. The day unfolded around them, the other pedestrians and commuters oblivious to the magic developing between these two individuals.

A safe and easy silence persisted as they walked together. Words seemed unnecessary, superfluous. They were already connected, their energetic bodies already familiar. Finally, Jason chose to speak.

"I, too, have been going through some really weird stuff," he revealed. "In fact, up until just the other day, I thought I was losing my mind."

Mary looked at Jason and studied his face. She detected no danger, no lurking malice, just the serious look of a man sharing a hard truth.

"I don't want to scare you, but something tells me we are going through a similar ordeal." Jason said.

Jason detected movement in his peripheral vision. He turned to face the street just in time to see the scowling, distorted face of a man hanging out of a pickup truck's passenger window. The man had something in his hand, which he threw directly at Jason as he howled, "Fuuuuckkkkk yoooouuuu!!!" The object was an egg, which hit Jason in the shoulder and splattered. The pickup truck sped off, its occupants laughing. Mary shrieked and covered her mouth. Jason simply stood there, covered in egg.

"Ever get the feeling someone's out to get you?" Jason joked.

"What was *that* all about?!? Are you *okay?*" Mary was shocked and perplexed. She started wiping egg off Jason's aching shoulder with her bare hands.

"I'm fine," Jason said. "This is fairly typical for me lately...although the egg is new. Nice touch, assholes."

A tall man in a business suit was approaching them on the sidewalk in a hurry. He was chattering excitedly on a cell phone and swinging a briefcase. Jason and Mary had to quickly step out of his way. The man was not stopping for anyone or anything.

As he passed, the man in the business suit said, presumably to whomever was on the other end of his phone, "Good shot! You got him. The woman's next..." The man hurriedly continued on his way, not once making eye contact with either Jason or Mary.

"Welcome to my world," Jason said, smiling despite having been assaulted moments ago. He was able, finally, to see the absurdity of the situation. It really was quite humorous.

A troubled expression appeared on Mary's face. Her eyes reflected deep, dark thoughts. "There's something you should know," she said. "I've been seeing a doctor because I was having paranoid, delusional thoughts – or at least I *thought* they were delusional...now I'm not so sure."

Jason offered his reassurance with a solemn nod. Mary continued:

"A few months ago, I started getting the feeling that I was being watched, stalked...targeted. Just weird coincidental stuff that's so hard to describe. Subtle, you know?"

"Yes. I *know.*".

"I couldn't figure out what I had done wrong, or who I had pissed off. It just seemed like suddenly the whole world was against me. It was worst online. I think my email was hacked and my activity tracked. Everywhere I went, I was harassed."

Mary was reliving a painful experience. Jason could see the hurt and bewilderment on her face. He wanted to make her feel loved and protected. The best he could do in the moment, without acting inappropriately or presumptuously, was to listen attentively and keep the communication open. They walked on, turning onto a tree-lined street in a quiet residential area.

"I think it all started when someone started a nasty rumor about me that spread among all my friends," Mary said. "I really don't even know the details, just that people started talking behind my back...mean, vicious stuff. It was like, within days, I had no friends left. They all abandoned me."

"It got worse," Mary continued. "When I went out, random strangers began whispering and pointing. I got dirty looks and seriously bad vibes everywhere I went...and like what just happened with that guy in the suit, I'd hear snippets of conversation that seemed to pertain directly to me or what I was experiencing. Even the movies and TV shows I watched seemed to contain references to my life!"

Mary shook her head and exhaled. Talking about her recent troubles was cathartic. "I was getting really paranoid," she said, "and when I tried to talk about it, people ignored me, dismissed me as totally crazy, or sometimes even reacted with hostility. My family wanted me to seek professional help, and eventually even *they* abandoned me. They stopped answering my calls and made it very clear that I was no longer welcome in their homes. They completely shut me out. Can you believe that?"

"Mary, I absolutely believe that. I went through the same exact thing. It's incredible how similar our experiences are."

"Well, I'll tell you, I became seriously depressed. It all

seemed to happen so fast. My life spun out of control. I thought the best thing I could do was leave town and start fresh somewhere new. I moved here, and guess what? The same shit started happening. I couldn't take it. I started seeing a psychiatrist."

"Did that help?"

"The doctor just wants me to take medication. I'm resistant to that. Seems like drugs would only help with the symptoms and mask the root cause."

"You got that right. Drugs will, in fact, make it much, much worse. Trust me."

"What is happening to us, Jason?".

"I don't know *exactly,* but it seems to me that we have been selected, targeted...I think that we are participants in an experiment or program of some sort. Figuring out what is happening and why might be the point of the game."

Jason looked directly into Mary's eyes, wild currents of electricity again passing between them. Jason spoke with an, until that moment, unknown passion:

"What is clear to me," he said, "is that we were meant to meet. We were brought together for a reason."

The conviction in his voice surprised him. Once spoken aloud, the words were strong magic. A powerful bond had been established between Jason and Mary. Together, their quest for truth would continue, their souls forged in the crucible of hardship, now eternally united.

It's always darkest before the dawn. Sometimes a cliché is a cliché because it works. Meeting each other – or reuniting, as the case may have been – was not the end of the tribulations for Jason and Mary. Reality was about to become even more unpredictable and erratic. The game still had some surprises in store for them.

"I feel like I've known you my entire life," Mary said

to Jason as they sat on the couch in his small apartment. They had only spent a few days together, but already they had grown extremely close. Jason was in love, he was sure of that. Mary was too, though she wasn't fully aware of the fact.

"I feel the same way," Jason said.

Prior to meeting, depression – solitary, smothering, and complete – had been their sole companion. Now they had each other, and in this transitory state, they existed in a wonderful bubble of new love, the early stages of which were filled with pure joy and total immersion in the present. Soon, the universe would once again pull them into the strange inner workings of the game, but for now, they were enjoying a brief respite.

They shared a quiet moment, comfortable, familiar, and secure. Time ceased and space pulled them along an unseen and inviolable trajectory, toward an inevitably alarming conclusion.

Enter once again, the forces of chaos.

From the street outside, where once a nightmarish chorus of honks and beeps had invaded Jason's sanctum and sanity, a high-pitched, shrieking noise rose in volume and pitch, piercing the walls of the apartment. It was loud, painful, and unsettling.

Mary put her hands over her ears. "Oh my god! What is *that?*"

The sound continued and her head started to throb in pain. Jason rubbed his forehead. He could actually *feel* his thoughts being disrupted.

"Ugh," Jason muttered. He got up and looked out the window. He could not see anything obviously causing the sound. "I'm going to go take a look," he said. "That's horrible." The pain was intensifying, his ability to think clearly diminishing.

Stepping out the door of the apartment building, Jason was struck by the bizarre non-locality of the sound. It seemed to be issuing from nowhere and everywhere somehow at once. Outside it *was* much louder, yet there was no clear source. Jason started to feel nauseated. His body trembled, his scalp tingled. It was extremely unpleasant.

It's a weapon, he thought.

The unmistakable smell of sulfur hung heavily in the air. There was a shimmering, hazy quality to the atmosphere, as if gas had been released in the neighborhood. Through the fog, Jason could see no cars and no other people. The street seemed to be entirely devoid of life, except for him. He stood surveying an empty world, like the sole survivor of the apocalypse.

The sound, for no apparent reason, began to wane. Jason was struck by the unreal nature of what he was perceiving. Instead of simply fading out, the high-pitched squeal seemed to be pulled or sucked out of the atmosphere. As it disappeared, there was a noticeable change in air pressure.

The world then seemed to return to 'normal.' The haze lifted and cars began appearing on the street again. Regular evening traffic resumed. Jason could even see pedestrians walking a block away. Jason was learning to accept high strangeness as a matter of routine, but that was an especially weird occurrence, and one that would be exceptionally difficult to describe to someone who had not been there to experience it.

Jason returned to his apartment. Mary was still sitting on his couch, a concerned look on her face. "What happened? Did you see anything?"

Jason struggled to find the words to explain what he had perceived. "It's weird out there," is all he could say. "But

I'm sure you already knew that."

A loud knock on the apartment door startled them both. They exchanged puzzled looks before Jason got up to see who it was. Peering through the eye hole, he saw an unfamiliar figure standing in the hall.

"Hello?" Jason said through the unopened door. "Who's there?"

The man was clean-cut, with an indistinct face, wearing a business suit and carrying a briefcase. *Is that the same man we encountered the other day?* Jason wondered. The man straightened his tie and looked directly into the eye hole. "I need to talk to you," the man said. "It's a matter of vital importance, both for you and the young lady."

"Who *are* you?" Jason asked.

"My name is Edward. I'm with the Bureau. You need to let me in. You need to talk to me."

Jason was suspicious...and *spooked.* He looked at Mary, who was shaking her head. *Don't trust him,* she mouthed silently. "I need to see some ID," Jason insisted.

"You *NEED* to let me in!" The man suddenly erupted in an angry outburst, his face instantly turning an unhealthy shade of red, spittle flying from his clenched jaw. *"OPEN THE DOOR NOW!"*

Stay calm, Jason thought. Mary got up from the couch and approached the eye hole. She looked through and took an abrupt step away from the door. "I've seen him before," she whispered. "We're calling the cops!" she yelled, addressing the man on the other side of the door. Her voice was strong and her will fierce.

"You're going to regret this," the man in the suit grumbled.

Jason watched through the eye hole as the man disappeared out of view and retreated down the hall. Silence.

There should have been a bang as the man exited the building through the heavy door. *Was he still out there?* Jason needed to know. His peace of mind depended on it.

Jason reluctantly opened the apartment door ever so slightly, preparing to defend himself from an imminent attack. The hall was empty. It was eerily silent and deserted. The man had apparently simply disappeared. "He's gone," Jason observed.

"We aren't safe here," Mary frowned. "We should leave. We'll take my car and leave town."

"Sounds like a good idea to me!"

Jason and Mary hastily gathered their essential belongings and left the apartment. As Jason locked the door, he had a premonition – he felt the sudden sensation that he would never again set foot in that apartment. The idea was not terribly upsetting to him. The apartment had been the arena for some of the most difficult trials of his entire life – it was the fiery furnace in which his soul had been forged.

They exited the building. Mary's car was waiting, gassed up and ready to take them away to the next stage of their adventure. They got in, with Mary as the driver and Jason the passenger.

"Well," Mary said. "Where to?"

"Let's just drive. Hit the highway and go where the spirit takes us. How does that sound?"

"Sounds exciting!" Mary grinned. She started up the car and they pulled out of the parking lot. As soon as they were on the road, it became apparent that leaving was not going to be a simple matter of driving away.

On a typical weekday evening, traffic would be light. This night, however, they were locked in congestion as soon as they hit the major streets. It was as if cars materialized out of nothingness and fell into place all around them, sealing them in and virtually preventing any movement whatsoever.

"What the heck?" Mary was astonished. "I've never seen anything like this. Where did all these cars come from?"

Jason knew the game still held them firmly it its grip. "Look at the drivers," he said as he pointed at a car directly beside them. Mary looked over...and gasped.

The face of the man in the driver's seat was a grotesque, distorted mass of indistinct features – shadows and flesh arranged in an inhuman mask. The man turned to face her and a gaping black hole opened in the center of his 'head.' A slimy, pink tongue-like appendage rolled out of the hole and twitched in an apparently taunting gesture.

"He's not *human!*" Mary stated the obvious.

More cars seemed to be merging with the heavy traffic, further sealing them in. Their car had nowhere to go – they had come to a full stop. The occupants of the other vehicles all had hideous demonic faces. An otherworldly fog had once again descended upon them, obscuring their vision beyond a few meters.

"We're trapped," Jason said, he too, stating the obvious. "I think we should get out of the car and walk."

"I don't know. What if those things attack?"

Jason had a flash of insight. "I don't think they can *physically* hurt us. They seem to be able to manipulate objects, but they themselves are ephemeral, inchoate."

Jason reached for the passenger door handle and prepared to step out. "I'm going to try something," he said.

"*Please* be careful," Mary urged. She watched him exit the vehicle, then with a sigh, decided to follow him.

Bumper-to-bumper gridlock traffic stretched for as far as they could see in the strange fog. Jason and Mary began walking up the street between vehicles. As they passed each car, the grotesque, deformed faces of the occupants turned to follow their progress.

Jason stopped at a random car – a small, white sedan, and bent over to peer into the side passenger window. A scowling creature lurched menacingly at him from behind the glass. Jason flinched, gathered his courage, and reached for the door handle. He somewhat expected it to be hot to the touch, or perhaps electrified, but it felt perfectly normal.

Jason opened the door...and the car became suddenly vacant. Billowy smoke hung in the car's interior, the smell of sulfur lingering in the stale air, but the occupants had vanished. Jason glanced back at Mary. "It just got a whole lot weirder," he deadpanned.

"Indeed," Mary nodded. She walked to the next car, smiled at the leering *thing* inside, and opened the door. Except for the unusual haze and the smell of sulfur, she found the interior empty.

"What *are* they?" Mary asked, mostly rhetorically. A voice spoke up from the other side of the car. It wasn't Jason's:

"They are exactly what they look like – *demons.*" There was a man standing by the driver's side door of the car Mary had just examined. He was an elderly gentleman with a large build and a kind, bespectacled face. "And they are as afraid of you as you are of them...more so, actually."

Jason joined Mary as the elderly man walked over to greet them. "My name is John," he said, extending a hand. They exchanged greetings and names. Jason and Mary were extremely relieved to encounter someone else who was apparently living in this bizarre, alternate reality.

John sized them up, assessing them with a critical but wise eye. "You should come with me," he said. "Safety in numbers and all that."

"How do we know we can trust you?" Jason asked,

although his instinct already told him that they could. Mary studied John's face, her own expression neutral.

Before John could answer, the door of a nearby SUV opened and a petite yet vibrant elderly woman exited and stood at John's side. She smiled warmly at Jason and Mary and took John's hand in her own. "You can trust us because we know what you are going through...and because John is the kindest, most generous man you will every meet."

"My wife, Sarah," John said. "Sarah, meet Jason and Mary." John allowed for a moment of pleasant introduction, and then spoke firmly: "Ok! Let's get this show on the road. We're being watched, you know." From the windows of every gridlocked car, they could see the drooling, demented faces of a legion of demonic entities peering back at them.

The foursome got into the SUV, the older couple in front, the younger in back.

"I can get us out of here," John said with confidence. Sure enough, he began to do just that. With expert (and aggressive) driving, he pulled forward and used the SUV to ram the vehicles directly in front of them out of the way. When he had enough room, he made a left hand turn and left the street entirely, driving instead through the front yards of the homes adjacent to the street.

John was thoroughly enjoying their little off-road excursion. "Oh *yeah!*" he exclaimed with pure joy as the SUV plowed forward, tearing up lawns and knocking over mailboxes.

"Someone's going to call the cops!" Mary yelled from the back seat. "What are you *doing?*"

"Young lady, I think it's safe to say that the cops aren't going to be much help to *anyone* any more," John replied. It was an ominous statement. Sarah looked at her husband with a serious, concerned countenance. "Don't scare them, honey."

"They can handle it." John cast a quick glance at the young couple in his rear-view mirror. "You can handle the truth, right? You wouldn't be here if you couldn't."

Jason reached over and grasped Mary's hand. He spoke for the two of them when he simply answered, "Yes."

"I thought so." John took a moment to gather his thoughts before continuing:

"What we are experiencing is a full-scale invasion by proxy of inhabitants of a parallel dimension. Let that sink in for a moment...it's a hard concept to swallow, I know."

It was more than a hard concept to swallow. It was a mind-blowing, paradigm-shattering neutron bomb of an idea. Jason and Mary sat in silence as they processed what John had just said. It was difficult.

"I was a professor of archaeology for many, many years," John went on, "and I've long been fascinated by the recurring tales of travelers – visitors, *invaders* – from other worlds, recorded in ancient texts and art. Some scholars dismiss stories of the archons, djinn, angels, demons, fairies, aliens, etc. as pure mythology or religious nonsense, but the stories are often very consistent, and appear in almost every ancient culture. It is my sincere belief that the events we are currently witnessing are the modern reappearance of these visitors...and, as I think we can all agree, the visitors are not friendly."

John's theory was so wild, so *out there*...yet it was hard to simply dismiss. For Jason, it had an uncanny familiarity, as if, somewhere deep in his subconscious, he already knew it to be the truth.

It was Mary who replied first. "You said it is an 'invasion by proxy'...what did you mean by that?"

"What I mean is that they are incorporeal – they don't have physical bodies, at least in our three-dimensional world

– but they can *influence* our world and, from what I've come to understand, actually inhabit the body of a human being. It's a disturbing thought, but it seems like they can wear people like suits and use them to exercise their will in this reality."

The SUV, still driving over lawns and driveways as a way of avoiding the gridlocked street, reached an intersection. They were now at the edge of town. A left turn would take them out of the city and into the surrounding countryside. A right turn would loop them back into the chaos.

Sarah, who had been quietly listening as John shared his interpretation of the bizarre situation, now spoke up: "It's time to make a decision. John and I are leaving the city. You two," she was referring to Jason and Mary, "are welcome to come with us. We have enough supplies to survive for many days in the wild while we consider our options and what to do next...or you can take your chances in town."

John turned to face the young couple, his expression serious, his eyes radiating concern and compassion. "You will continue to be targeted, no matter where you go – you can't escape those things – but perhaps if we combine our talents and resources we can find some answers. We should stick together. Come with us."

"There's one thing I know for sure," Jason said, breaking his contemplative silence. "I have no desire to go back to my apartment. That place is a hellhole...*literally.*"

"There would be no love lost between me and this town," Mary said, "and there's so much more I need to know...why we were targeted, for example. I don't really understand. If those...*entities*...can 'possess' people, then why not us?"

John smiled. "That's the question of the hour, Mary. I

think together we can find the answer." He gestured with his head toward the open highway leading out of town. "Shall we?"

Jason and Mary exchanged a quick glance, agreement and excitement clearly visible on their faces. "Let's do it," Mary said.

"Sounds like a good plan to me," Jason agreed.

"Excellent," Sarah said.

"Huzzah!" John cheered.

The SUV turned onto the highway. The open road and the great unknown opened up to receive the intrepid foursome.

With John still behind the wheel, the group drove through the night. The world was cloaked in darkness. High beams pierced the black shroud, illuminating only the road directly ahead of the SUV. Reality had contracted into a small bubble encapsulating only the interior of the vehicle. Muted voices partook in quiet conversation.

"I've seen some truly remarkable artifacts and relics," John said, his voice conveying reverence. "Representations of the entities. Some cultures depict them as reptilian or draconian, some depict them as giants. I've seen carvings of elf-like creatures straight out of a Disney movie. What I've come to believe is that they can take on any form they wish. They are ultra-dimensional creatures...if they are indeed creatures at all. They could very well be pure, malevolent, non-localized consciousness."

"Well, that sure was a mouthful," Jason said. He and Mary, who had her head on his shoulders and her eyes closed, were exhausted. They had been through an ordeal in their short time together.

"Imagine living with him," Sarah joked. "I hear this stuff every day." She leaned over and gave her husband a small kiss on the cheek. "But I love him. He has a good heart."

Sarah's speech took on a thoughtful tone. "I wonder, though, if these events aren't eschatological in nature. It's hard not to notice similarities to the end times scenarios in various religious traditions."

"That's an interesting perspective," John said, pondering the idea. "Are you saying this is the final judgment?"

"I don't know about *that,*" Sarah replied, "but I remember you saying there's a spiritual element to the phenomenon."

Jason listened intently to what the older couple was saying, and something occurred to him. His troubles, he realized, began when he immersed himself in philosophical study. It was during his sincere and passionate pursuit of truth – the greater truth of his existence – that he had become a target. The timing was significant.

"I think there's something to that, Sarah," Jason said. "You were right, John, when you said the demons fear us. People like us are probably their greatest threat. We think, we feel, we search for meaning and understand that life has *purpose.* It prevents us from being directly consumed, but it makes us targets. The invaders are forced to resort to other means of attacking us. In my case – as in many others, I'm sure – they tried to drive me crazy."

Mary was fully alert now, carefully following the conversation. "Me too," she said. "I went through the very same thing...and it all seemed to start when I began unplugging from the BS – the everyday crap that just started to get me down. It was like I could no longer relate to those around me. Do you know what I mean?"

The other occupants of the vehicle nodded in unanimous, vehement agreement.

"People are so vain and foolish sometimes," Mary continued. "Cell phones, 'selfies,' tattoos, promiscuity, rampant drug and alcohol abuse, violence glorified and brutality embraced...it's a mean, weird world and I just don't know if I belong in it. Maybe I'm just sensitive and naive."

"The qualities that make you a target are also the qualities that make you a wonderful person, my dear," Sarah smiled. "Kindness, compassion, thoughtfulness, humility – beautiful and rare attributes."

"I hate to interrupt the conversation," John said, "but, unfortunately, we are very low on gas. I'm going to have to stop at the next station."

The foursome drove for a few more miles before the lights of a service station appeared just ahead. Taking the next exit, the SUV pulled into the lot. The station was small – four pumps and a small convenience store – and it was eerily quiet. Though the lights were on and the pumps appeared functional, there were no other cars and, seemingly, no other people.

John got out of the vehicle first. He surveyed the scene and was struck by the sense of abandonment that pervaded and the ominous, haunted atmosphere. "I don't see anyone here," he shouted to the others, who waited in the SUV.

John approached the pump. It had a credit card slot. John retrieved a card from his wallet, inserted it into the slot, and was relieved to see text on the LED screen indicate that the pump was ready for use. He began fueling the large vehicle.

There were lights on in the store, which was little more than a large kiosk. "Who's hungry?" John asked his companions. Judging by the excited murmuring, *everyone* was hungry.

"I'll go get snacks," Jason offered.

"I'll go with you," Mary said. "Would you like something, Sarah?"

"I'm fine, thank you," Sarah replied. She was relaxed and seated comfortably, with no desire to eat or move. "I need to rest."

The young couple hopped out of the vehicle and walked up to the store's entrance. Upon entering, an extremely unpleasant odor immediately caused the pair to recoil in disgust. It was the unmistakable smell of rotting meat.

"Oh my *God*," Mary gagged. "What stinks?!"

"A problem with the cooler, probably," Jason grimaced. "Smells like meat going bad."

The store was tiny, large enough only for four or five racks of typical convenience store fare – chocolate bars, potato chips, candy and other highly processed junk foods. A cooler unit occupied the wall opposite the door. There did not appear to be anyone else in the store.

Jason and Mary cautiously navigated the narrow aisles, making their way to the beverage cooler. "Let's get some drinks and snacks and get out of here," Jason muttered. "I'll just leave some money on the counter to cover what we take."

"This place is creepy," Mary said. "Let's get our stuff and *go!*"

As they gathered items, a noise directed their attention to the cashier's station. Jason and Mary froze in position, thoroughly and completely spooked. There was something behind the counter, out of view. Rustling, munching sounds of a truly disturbing quality filled the air.

Jason summoned his courage and took a step forward. Mary put a hand on his shoulder and joined him as he approached the source of the unnerving sounds. Reaching the counter, Jason peered over to get a look behind, and found himself face to face with a living nightmare.

It was a scene of utter carnage. It took a moment for Jason's brain to register what he was seeing. He could, at first, only perceive violence and blood – a lot of blood – splattered and pooled everywhere in ugly shades of brown and red. "Fuck!" he yelled, jumping back.

Before Jason could warn her, Mary too looked behind the counter. "He's *eating* him!" she shrieked.

She was right about that. Behind the counter, a man was feeding on the face of another, presumably dead, man. The eater looked up and grinned in total madness. Bits of partially chewed flesh and rivulets of blood cascaded out of his twisted mouth. "God is real! Help! Help! Real! *This is hell!* Don't make me eat you!" he screamed as Jason and Mary ran out of the store.

John saw them coming and could sense their fear and panic. "What's going on?" he asked as he replaced the pump nozzle.

"We have to go *now!*" Jason yelled.

John asked no more questions. They jumped into the SUV and John quickly started the engine. Lights appeared on the highway – many lights, approaching from the direction from which they had come. It was as if a hundred-car convoy was rolling down the highway. Before the group in the SUV could get out of the service station parking lot and back on the highway, cars began pulling in, converging on their location.

"We've got serious company," Sarah observed, as a procession of cars poured into the service station lot and surrounded the SUV. Once again, they were trapped. An impenetrable perimeter had formed around them, supernaturally organized and executed. The occupants of the other vehicles had distorted, demonic visages.

"Well, friends," John said. "We are in a real pickle now."

"Let's walk," Jason suggested.

"Where?" Mary asked. "We're totally surrounded...and what if they attack?"

"Have faith," Sarah said, stepping out of the vehicle. The SUV was illuminated by the focused headlights of the other vehicles which encircled it. Sarah stood in the spotlight, emboldened by a renewed sense of purpose. It had become clear to her that they were engaged in spiritual warfare...and her spirit was *strong*.

"Join me," she encouraged her companions in the SUV. "They can't hurt you."

John, Jason, and Mary took their places at her side. At once, every car in the demonic battalion blared its horn in a cacophonous chorus. The din was bone-shaking and skull-rupturing, and sliced right to the soul of each individual in the circle. The hideously disfigured drivers sneered and howled in delirium. The cornered foursome stood their ground.

Sarah addressed the demons. She repeated what she said to her friends: "Join me."

A most unusual and unexpected thing happened – many did, in fact, join her. As the small group in the center of the circle watched, car doors began to open. People of all ages, genders, and races stepped out of the vehicles and congregated in the circle, their appearances human once more. One-third of the demons had heard Sarah's call – and answered it.

"Welcome back," John said.

It was Mary who first noticed the faint light appearing on the horizon. Morning had come, a soft orange light beginning to seep into the darkness of the night sky. "The sun is coming up," she said.

It was a fair statement, a reasonable assessment. As the group observed, however, it was soon obvious that the explanation for what they were witnessing was much stranger than that. Something was happening in the sky, and it wasn't a simple sunrise.

Warm shades of red and orange continued to bleed into the sky, but in a hallucinatory, kaleidoscopic fashion. It was like watching a massive lava lamp in the heavens. The foursome was mesmerized. Over their heads, pools of iridescent fluid seemed to be forming and spreading. What appeared to be distant lightning flashed at various, random places in the sky. A deep rumbling sound emanated from the very depths of the abyss. The ground trembled.

The demons, too, were enthralled by the event. They craned their heads to look up at the sky, drooling and panting like demented idiots. What was happening was *momentous.*

With a loud crack of electricity and a burst of high energy particles, a rift appeared. The sky split like torn fabric, revealing the Great Beyond in all its ineffable glory. John, Sarah, Mary, and John gazed through the hole in reality into another dimension, transfixed...transfigured. Great pillars of flame spewed forth, consuming the monstrous entities and their vehicles like tongues of wrath. The screams of the damned reverberated in the fiery maelstrom as the creatures were immolated.

The foursome, and those who had left their vehicles to join them, stood amid the destruction untouched. A mighty hand, impossibly large and difficult to fathom, reached through the rift, the span of its fingers obscuring the sky. It descended upon them, but before the immense appendage blotted out their view of the world beyond, a giant eye was briefly visible, framed by the gateway, and sparkling with infinite intelligence and compassion. The assembled group of survivors raised their faces to the wondrous spectacle, their minds clear and free, their hearts mirroring the beauty and grandeur of the portal.